Ichimei
Tsukushi

ILLUSTRATION BY

Enji

2

Dragon
and Ceremony
The
Passing of
the Witch

CONTENTS

PROLOGUE ———————————————— 001

CHAPTER 1 **The Witch Lives in the Forest** ———————— 013

CHAPTER 2 **The Witch Eats People** ——— 047

CHAPTER 3 **The Witch Lives** ——————— 097

CHAPTER 4 **The Witch Is Gone** ———— 153

EPILOGUE ———————————————— 195

DRAGON AND CEREMONY

Presented by Ichimei Tsukushi

Dragon and Ceremony

The Passing of the Witch

2

Ichimei Tsukushi

ILLUSTRATION BY **Enji**

YEN ON

New York

DRAGON AND CEREMONY
ICHIMEI TSUKUSHI

Translation by Jordan Taylor
Cover art by Enji

RYU TO SAIREI Vol. 2 -DENSHOU SURU MAJO-
Copyright © 2020 Ichimei Tsukushi
Illustrations copyright © 2020 Enji
All rights reserved.
Original Japanese edition published in 2020 by SB Creative Corp.

This English edition is published by arrangement with SB Creative Corp., Tokyo in care of Tuttle-Mori Agency, Inc., Tokyo.

English translation © 2022 by Yen Press, LLC

Yen On
150 West 30th Street, 19th Floor
New York, NY 10001

Visit us at yenpress.com
facebook.com/yenpress
twitter.com/yenpress
yenpress.tumblr.com
instagram.com/yenpress

First Yen On Edition: May 2022

Yen On is an imprint of Yen Press, LLC.
The Yen On name and logo are trademarks of Yen Press, LLC.

Library of Congress Cataloging-in-Publication Data
Names: Tsukushi, Ichimei, author. | Enji, illustrator. | Taylor, Jordan (Translator), translator.
Title: Dragon and ceremony / Ichimei Tsukushi ; illustration by Enji ; translation by Jordan Taylor.
Other titles: Ryū to sairei. English
Description: First Yen On edition. | New York, NY : Yen On, 2022–
Identifiers: LCCN 2021046140 | ISBN 9781975336936 (v. 1 ; trade paperback.) | ISBN 9781975336950 (v. 2 ; trade paperback) | ISBN 9781975336974 (v. 3 ; trade paperback)
Subjects: CYAC: Fantasy. | Dragons—Fiction. | Quests (Expeditions)—Fiction. | LCGFT: Fantasy fiction. | Light novels.
Classification: LCC PZ7.1.T7826 Dr 2022 | DDC [Fic]—dc23
LC record available at https://lccn.loc.gov/2021046140

ISBNs: 978-1-9753-3695-0 (paperback)
        978-1-9753-3696-7 (ebook)

10 9 8 7 6 5 4 3 2 1

LSC-C

Printed in the United States of America

She couldn't join the ring of dancing people. They told her she wasn't the right age to participate, then spared her not a single glance after that as they danced across the harvested fields. In truth, she should have been able to dance alongside them. There were children younger than her among those who leaped and spun.

What was wrong? One of the adults asked her. Wasn't she going to go dance? Did her tummy hurt? She slapped aside the outstretched hand and fell farther behind the crowd.

Adults had been kids once, so she'd believed they would get what it was like to be one. So why couldn't they understand? Perhaps, just as there weren't any children who could remember what happened before they were born, there weren't any adults who could remember what happened before they grew up. Simple as that.

She looked out at the fields in silence.

She didn't want to think about jealousy or hate.

No, she wanted to watch them dancing, not a thought in her mind.

Just then, a shadow fell into view.

She blinked.

In the direction of the ring of dancers, who were moving faster and faster. On the far side of the field.

There stood a black figure.

For a while, she thought she was the only one who could see it. Neither the young dancers nor the nearby adults noticed.

A cold droplet fell on her nose.

She looked up to find raindrops falling from ashen clouds.

Before she could even register that it was pouring, a white light filled her vision, and a roar ripped through the sky.

The only thing not washed out in that world of white light was the black figure. It stood out in stark contrast.

"Witch."

Said someone.

The witch. The witch was here. The witch had come.

Fear spread from person to person, and it even seemed to reach the clouds as rain fell in a deluge to the earth.

Adults and children alike panicked, mud coating them as they rushed as far away as possible. Their terror-stricken faces and screams were lost behind the downpour.

Only the one girl remained; she crossed the field.

As she walked, she felt the unpleasant squelching of mud beneath her feet. Despite almost getting trapped a few times, she continued straight ahead.

As she approached the black figure, she noticed that they were staring at her...or so she felt. The figure was so much taller than her that she could barely make out their face.

"Are you the witch?" the girl asked.

The elements nearly drowned out the sound of her own voice, but for some reason, she could clearly make out the figure's reply.

"I am."

"You made it rain, didn't you?"

"Me?" said the witch in amusement. "Why would I do something like that? Aren't you the one who made it rain?"

"Why do you think that?"

"Because of the face you're making."

With that, she realized the witch was teasing her.

"Where do you live?" asked the girl.

"In the forest."

"...Take me with you."

"Hmm, are you sure?"

"Why wouldn't I be?"

"Don't you know?" Their mouth curved up into a crescent. "Witches eat humans."

"Really?"

"Oh? You're not scared?"

"Nuh-uh."

"Hmm. Then you may accompany me."

"Okay."

"But are you really sure?"

"I don't mind. Besides..."

If she got eaten, she wouldn't worry about anything anymore.

After all, when you died, surely you would forget everything that happened to you before that.

○

Ix had expected to find an overwhelming crowd in the capital, but it wasn't that different from the level of traffic in Leirest. He did notice, however, that he was seeing different sorts of faces here. Or perhaps it was better to say faces with a different destination.

The people who came to Leirest were merchants or travelers, and they weren't going to end their journeys there. The city was just a waypoint, a place for people to rest on the road to their real destinations. The most common type of person to pass through its gates was a merchant, who earned money by moving goods from town to town. These folks rarely gave much consideration to the areas they were currently in. Instead, they seemed to always have their minds on the town they would be visiting next.

In that respect, the capital was different. It was the end of the line for the people who arrived there. Even if it would serve as the start of another journey someday, for the time being, it was their final destination. Thoughts of the next town in on the road vanished from the minds of travelers there. In the capital, they focused only on the place they were in. Perhaps that was what made all the people passing by on the streets seem relaxed. And indeed, despite the huge throngs in the streets, no one seemed rushed.

Ix sat by a window, people watching.

He was in an expensive room, waiting for someone.

A new customer came through the door. An immaculate store employee approached them with silent steps, making idle chitchat as they led the customer into a back room. There, a number of staffs and wands for sale were on display. Ix had looked them over earlier, and they were all of the highest quality.

Ix thought it would have been better to set up the store so that customers went straight into the showroom when they entered, but perhaps the room up front was used for something else. Lavishly decorated, it had several desks and chairs lined along the walls, each set spaced out from the others. There was no one sitting in the room besides Ix, just quite a number of shop workers standing at the ready for any new customers who might walk in the door. Ix sat in the back of the room.

"Mr. Ix," came a voice.

It belonged to a young man in a work uniform. When Ix turned to face him, the man bade him to follow along, then opened a door to another chamber.

They passed several rooms in the back, such as a storage room for equipment that wasn't regularly used and a room where even more employees were silently toiling away. Ix had only a quick glance at them, but he decided they all seemed to be well-experienced wandmakers. Since he was just an apprentice, he wouldn't be able to hold a candle to them.

They continued deep into the building until the man came to a stop in front of a heavy-looking door. He turned back to Ix and told him to wait.

"Can't you just open it?" Ix asked the man, who was standing by the entrance.

"I am unable to."

"Uh-huh."

Suddenly, the door swung open, and much more lightly than one would expect at that.

A cloying perfume assaulted Ix's nostrils.

The chamber inside was dimly lit. There were no windows, and the only light was from a few candles. As the door opened, it created a draft that sent their flames flickering. The decorations were incredibly gaudy, and the whole place was slathered in reds and golds. It would have dazzled the eyes had it been fully lit.

A massive bed sat in the center of the room, it, too, in a lurid red and gold. Gauzelike curtains cascaded around the bed, blocking the inside from sight.

Ix unceremoniously swiped the curtains aside, and the woman in bed stirred.

"It's me," he said.

"You've come a long way," came a muffled voice.

It was muffled because she was wearing a mask.

The mask wasn't the kind that only covered the area around your eyes. In fact, it was far larger than the wearer's face. Elongated and ovular, it stretched up and down at an angle. It was crafted of wood that had been painted white, with a face drawn on using tribal patterns. Her voice emanated from behind it.

The mask wasn't the only strange thing about the woman. Although she was sitting upright, her vivid red hair spread out all across the bed, so long that it hung over the edge. Instead of bedclothes, she was dressed in high-end clothing that looked as though she was about to attend a noble's ball, right down to the inordinate amount of jewelry dangling from her wrists and neck. Beside her, an incense burner let out white smoke, the kind that gradually made your mind go hazy.

Ix shook his head and looked down at her.

"Why'd you call me here?" he asked.

The woman was called Layumatah, the most senior of

Munzil's apprentices. She gracefully gestured toward the edge of the bed with a gentle clink of metal on metal.

"Sit," she said slowly.

"I'm fine standing."

"Sit."

"I'm—"

"Sit."

"……"

Ix took a seat on the edge of the bed. It was unbelievably soft. The mattress sank beneath his weight, and some of Layumatah's hair brushed the ground.

As the most junior of all the apprentices, Ix had no right to go against the eldest. With their master dead, she now held the most authority over him.

He sat with his hands on his knees, only his upper body turned toward her.

"I hear you're not making wands," she remarked.

"How would you know that?"

"Morna told me."

Morna was Layumatah's junior and Ix's senior. She was also the craftswoman for the store where he was currently staying.

"...Uh-huh," Ix replied.

"And why aren't you?"

"'Cause I don't have any reason to make any, I guess. The shop doesn't need any more craftspeople. Morna makes way better wands than I do, so I'm just staying out of her way."

"That girl is a genius. If the excuse you just gave was valid, you would go your entire life without making a wand. In fact, by that logic, no one but the single most skilled craftsman would have cause to make a wand. Is that what you meant to say?"

"...Who even cares about why people make wands?" Truth was, however, that he was probably stuck in this rut *because* he lacked a reason to practice his craft. "So you going to give me advice or something?"

"Of course not. Why would I help you?"

"Then cut to the chase. Why'd you call me all the way out here to the capital?"

"The wand wall has been undone."

"Huh…?" The simplicity of the statement left Ix dumbfounded. "The wand wall? Wh-which one? It broke?" he asked, his tone unintentionally growing stronger.

"Here, of course. The capital's wand wall. It hasn't been broken. And while I said it has been undone, even that is not a certainty. Thus far, all we have is the discovery of a secret document that claims as much."

"Huh?"

"A guard at the city gate found it concealed in a merchant's cargo. But even the merchant didn't know it had been hidden there. Since the merchant travels the same route regularly, they were likely just a convenient mule. The document has been inspected, but there are no to or from names. That merchant won't be used again to transport such things, since the secret document was found. They should have let it continue on; it was foolish of them to stop it."

According to what Layumatah said, whoever wrote this document claimed to have discovered a method to undo the capital's wand wall.

A wand wall was a specialized structure built into the walls of a city. Put simply, it was just a massive wand in its own right. An entire tree trunk would be worked into a wand-like shape and embedded into the barrier's interior. If there was ever an attack on the city, the wand wall would be activated to increase the strength of the city's fortifications. Although there were weapons that could counter these devices, known as siege wands, that didn't change the fact that wand walls were essential for defense.

Generally, each wand wall was equipped with a safety feature known as a lock, which acted as a sort of code. Locks could be undone through a specific process, which would nullify all the wand wall's capabilities. This was apparently put in place as a safeguard in case a rebellion took over a city. But even the person who installed the lock didn't have the knowledge to undo it—only a select few government officials were privy to this.

Suspicious, Ix asked, "Sure it's not just some bad prank?"

"The secret document also detailed other security issues within the capital. They were all confidential, yet I am told almost none of the information in the document was incorrect."

"Seriously? This is the capital's wand wall we're talking about. That's not your everyday problem. You could probably gather a whole conference worth of craftsmen to debate the issue, and they'd still draw a blank. I find it hard to believe someone could secretly investigate and undo—"

"Do you really think no one else drew the same conclusion as you?" countered Layumatah quickly. "That argument has already been dismissed. A decision has been made. Security will temporarily be increased in the capital while a new lock is made. I have been put in charge of that."

"…Uh-huh."

Well, if she was leading the project, it wouldn't even matter much if the old lock had been dismantled. The new one would provide security for at least another hundred years.

However, there was still a *but* on Layumatah's lips.

"There is something that still bothers me," she admitted.

"It's not often you don't understand something."

"I didn't say I don't understand it; I said it bothers me." Her body hardly moved as she spoke. It was like speaking with a ventriloquist. "I've examined the wand wall's designs in the course of my work. It has been repaired on the several occasions it was installed, and its most recent mending took place approximately sixty years ago. That time, they used the emission method."

"Well, that's a standard procedure… Wait." Ix opened a hand. "Didn't using the emission method only become commonplace around thirty years ago?"

"That same thing occurred to me. I looked into it but found that was indeed the procedure they used."

"Did the kingdom hide the technique? No, even if they did, they would have used it on military wands before it found its way to the public..."

"I did not ask for your speculation. Regardless of what went on back then, there was a person who designed the emission method sixty years ago. And I suspect it's that same individual who's undone the lock now."

"Ah... I see."

Deactivating a wand wall's lock was an incredibly difficult task. But if someone had been involved in working on it in the past and comprehended enough to be able to design the emission method sixty years ago, they might just have been able to do it.

"After investigating further," continued Layumatah, "I discovered there was one name among those who worked on the wall that didn't belong to a craftsman: Mali, a noblewoman. It wouldn't have been strange for an aristocrat to participate in name alone, but there are very few records about this lady. It's strange. You would expect her to take credit for the project." Layumatah raised her right arm and pointed at Ix. "I order you to investigate her."

"...What?"

"Investigate Mali and report back to me."

"Wh-what the hell?" Ix couldn't stop himself from standing up. "I don't get it. This is the first time I'm hearing about this woman. How am I supposed to investigate her? Besides, isn't this the kind of request you give to an adventurer? Why ask me?"

"I heard you're adept at this kind of investigation."

"Who would have—?"

"Morna told me."

Flashing an exceedingly bitter look, Ix sat back down on the bed.

Even so, this conversation was generally playing out how he'd suspected. Layumatah wouldn't have invited him to the capital for no reason. He'd assumed she would have an appropriate job of sorts to give him. But he hadn't exactly expected to find himself investigating an unfamiliar noblewoman.

"You will likely need assistance, so I have arranged for some help. Take them with you," said Layumatah.

"Help? You're sending a shop employee off, too?"

"They're under my jurisdiction. I wouldn't just lend them to you."

A furrow appeared on Ix's brow as he wondered if they were going to be some random adventurer, then. He'd avoided the Adventurers' Guild ever since those two adventurers had beat him up out of revenge.

"Time limit?" he asked.

"None. But you must return your assistant by autumn, and it will be more difficult to act once winter comes and the snow falls. Send a report before then. I expect a good one."

"Don't be ridiculous," hissed Ix, making no effort to hide his complaint. Not that he expected Layumatah to listen.

As he sat there thinking of at least one way he would resist her, she turned her stare—from behind her mask—toward him.

"Something else—?" he began.

"Witch."

"Huh?"

"Witch," Layumatah said again. "Master told me a witch made it. This happened before I finished my apprenticeship. I asked him about the capital's wand wall, and he told me, *'That was made by a witch. Humans can't learn from that thing.'* I assumed he was just spouting random nonsense again, so I forgot about it until this incident occurred. Perhaps what he said was true." Layumatah's mask turned up slightly. "Have you heard that before?"

Ix shook his head wordlessly.

Witch. It was the first time the word had ever crossed his ears. If a witch could make the wand wall, perhaps they were some kind of magic user or craftsman? Though it was a mystery to him why they would need a special term. Perhaps it was because they were some sort of special being? If it was related to this incident, that meant this noblewoman Mali could be one...

"Sixty years ago, yeah? If she was the witch, we'll be lucky if she's still alive," said Ix.

"Master said witches are immortal."

"Huh?"

"But in exchange for their endless life, they have to eat humans."

"Huh? What the hell is that?"

Ix shrugged at the absurdity of it all.

He could vaguely understand people putting some powerful being on a pedestal, but when you threw in immortality and cannibalism, it made the whole thing seem like something out of a folktale.

"Layumatah, you can't be saying you actually believe this stuff?"

"I am simply recounting to you what I heard. What I believe or don't believe has no bearing on reality," she replied coldly. "I have confirmed two things: that Mali still lives and her current location."

"If you know that much, just go yourself."

"I'm giving you this task since she's closest to you."

"Closest? So she's in Leirest?"

"Mali Saneeld. She is the current head of the Leirest Library."

"She's the head librarian...?"

"Do you know her?"

"Guess you could say that."

"I see. Well, off you go, then," she ordered, raising her chin toward the door.

"......"

As he went to leave the room, she called out to him again.

"Ix."

He turned back but said nothing.

The mask was facing him.

"Do you remember the first staff you ever made?"

CHAPTER 1

The Witch Lives in the Forest

1

Ix was expelled from Layumatah's shop like bile from a vomiting beast.

He rarely ever had any contact with her, but the few interactions they did have always left him exhausted. That was partially the fault of her being the most senior apprentice of Munzil's and he the most junior, but it mostly came down to the fact that he felt as though she were staring right through him whenever they spoke.

Just as Munzil had limitations in certain areas, all his apprentices had their own as well, and they were often extreme. Ix, for instance, lacked magic, while Morna had no interpersonal skills. And Layumatah, the most senior, was blind.

Ix didn't know if she'd been born without sight or she'd lost it from a disease. He'd even heard whispers that once she became Munzil's apprentice, she blinded herself after realizing her vision would just be a hindrance. He couldn't tell which was the truth, but regardless, her other senses were exceedingly sharp. She was of course an excellent wandmaker, but she also excelled at evaluating people. Out of all Munzil's apprentices, she was the only one capable of running a large-scale shop like this, and probably the only one who would even consider doing so.

Now that I think about it...

Ix frowned.

Like her, had he gained some skill in place of having magic?

Apparently, before Munzil died, he had said that Ix was the most talented of his apprentices, supposedly because he was the only one who could view wandmaking from the outside. But that was so abstract. It was true, however, that humans without magic were incredibly rare. Ix wasn't aware of anyone like that besides himself. Still, he'd never considered the possibility that he might have gained something else in exchange. It wasn't even clear how Ix was still alive. Perhaps he did have something special, some sort of talent...

Dark, heavy clouds hung in the sky, typical of the kingdom around this time of year.

Ix had agreed to meet this assistant that Layumatah had arranged at the Marayist cathedral. It wasn't close to the shop, but he wasn't worried about getting lost. All he had to do was head for the tallest building that wasn't the castle.

Marayism was a widely followed religion in the kingdom, as the king was also the head of the church. As Ix came closer to the cathedral, the streets became increasingly crowded with believers flocking there to worship. Many of them were dressed in traveling garb; perhaps they were pilgrims from distant lands.

Though the cathedral was majestic from a distance, it was even more overwhelming up close. Its spires seemed to pierce the heavens, and the carvings on its walls barely looked like they were made of stone. Ix couldn't imagine how long it would have taken to build. After hesitating, he slipped quietly inside and walked along the edge of the nave.

The structure seemed even more absurd to him as he examined the interior decorations. Every single detail was extraordinary. From the religious scenes painted on the ceilings to the stained glass windows, all the ornamentations were the telltale products of zealous craftsmen. Apparently, the cathedral had been finished more than two hundred years ago.

At the moment, a priest was standing at the pulpit, preaching about something in a sonorous voice. Followers gathered around him, listening. Ix also saw the occasional person off by themselves praying and small groups standing near the entrance chatting. Surprisingly, it seemed they were free to do as they wished.

Ix went toward a pillar with engravings of a five-legged beast as he'd been instructed and found that someone was already standing there. As he approached, they turned to look at him.

She was a young woman, or perhaps even a girl. Her bangs were so long that they hid her eyes, and her loose-fitting outfit was lengthy enough to sweep the ground. She was slightly petite, but not so much so that she stood out. Overall, she came across as rather plain and timid.

"You the help Layumatah requested?" asked Ix.

"Yes," she replied in a quiet but high-pitched voice.

"I'm Ix."

"I'm…Nova."

"You look pretty young."

"You…think so?"

"…How old are you?"

"Eighteen."

"You a student?"

"Yes."

"At the Academy?"

"Yes."

The conversation petered off there. She seemed to lack energy, which suited her appearance. That wasn't something you should judge a person for, but Ix was completely befuddled as to why Layumatah would choose this girl. Perhaps she'd just picked out a student who had nothing else going on? On second thought, though, she would be easier to deal with than some chatterbox. He was going to be spending the next couple of weeks with her, after all.

Suddenly, Nova turned toward the pulpit. The priest was still speaking in calm tones. His voice echoed up into the high ceiling; at this distance, his sermon's message was impossible to make out.

In a hushed voice, Nova said, "The sermon, just now."

"Huh?"

"There are no, matching texts. The priest seems to be, mixing proverbs and, scripture. It is easy to understand, but needs further explanation, I think." She had a peculiar way of speaking where she paused every few words, but it wasn't too hard on the ears.

"...Why did you say to meet in the cathedral?" asked Ix.

"Many people come and go, so we wouldn't be conspicuous here. There are few places to hide, except for behind the pillars, so we wouldn't have to worry about people overhearing."

"You know what the job is?"

"Yes." Her bangs swayed as she nodded. "We are to investigate, a woman named Mali."

"I'm not sure if it's my place to ask, but why'd you accept this assignment? I'm not the one deciding, but the story itself sounds pretty fishy, and the job doesn't sound particularly interesting. You in it for the money?"

"Money, and my own interests, are irrelevant. I am simply, accompanying."

"So you're just tagging along, then?"

Suddenly, Nova veered off topic. "There, now."

"Huh? What?"

She pointed toward the entrance.

Amid the crowds of worshippers stood a person wearing a gray coat. They slipped through and entered the cathedral. Their head was pulled down far so you couldn't see their face. Just as Ix had done, the figure walked along the edge of the nave, almost blending into the shadows as they continued in Nova and Ix's direction. Their steps were soundless; they seemed to be making a conscious effort not to stand out.

Ix's eyes locked on to the figure simply because he knew someone who dressed just like that. Well, wearing a gray coat wasn't particularly unusual in itself. Regardless, one look at her was all he needed to figure out who she was.

As she approached Ix and Nova, the person in the coat said quietly, "Oh, Nova, is that you?"

"Yes," the girl replied.

"I was told someone else was coming, but I didn't realize it would be you... Well, I look forward to working together."

"Me too."

"And"—she turned toward Ix—"long time no see, Ix."

"...How's the wand?" he asked in response.

"That is your first concern? How very you."

Now here was someone who was difficult to deal with.

But also just who he needed.

2

Ix hadn't seen Yuui Laika since he'd repaired her wand over the summer.

He couldn't discern her face, concealed by the hood as it was, but there was a moment of silence, so he suspected she was sighing.

"Yes, the wand. There have been no issues. It performed wonderfully at the exam I had the other day," confirmed Yuui.

"That's good," he replied.

"And how are you, Ix?"

"Same as always."

"I'm happy to hear that." Yuui shot a brief glance at Nova. She was looking at Yuui in confusion but seemed to generally avoid speaking unless she was spoken to.

"You two friends?" asked Ix.

"I suppose you could say that... Though the explanation would take too long, so let's just say for now that we are classmates. Layumatah has asked me to help the two of you."

"There won't be any problems with you both not going to class?" asked Ix.

©Enji

"No," clarified Nova curtly.

"It won't change how they treat me like a failure," added Yuui as she fiddled with her hood.

Yuui Laika was in a very complicated situation in the kingdom. She was not a citizen, but rather a girl who'd been abducted from the small country of Lukutta, which the kingdom had invaded. She was currently attending the Royal Academy, but that wasn't of her own volition. It would be more accurate to call her a hostage than a student.

The sermon seemed to draw to a close, and the priest's reverberating voice halted. The attendees dispersed, intentionally making a fuss as they did. The three put their conversation on hold as they waited for the crowd to leave.

However, a man broke off from the group moving toward the exit and called over to them.

"Oh, is that you, Nova?" he said. This man wore the same religious vestments as the priest who had given the sermon, but he was younger. "Ah, so it is. What a coincidence."

"Father," said Nova quietly.

"Are these classmates of yours?" asked the man.

"Something, like that."

"Why are you hiding your face?" he asked, glancing at Yuui in confusion.

"I have a rash," she replied without hesitation.

"Oh, sorry. Uh, have you come to pray?"

"I am showing these two, the cathedral," said Nova.

"Ah, how wonderful. This building vies for the position of first- or second-most historical building in the kingdom. Its scale is, of course, part of that, but each and every one of the carvings contains a clear message. For example, the pillar that you three are standing next to—" he told them, pointing to the carvings of the five-legged beasts. "Ah, my apologies. If I do all the explaining, I'll be stealing the opportunity from you, Nova."

"Thank you."

"Anyway, please do take your time looking around." The man went to leave but quickly turned back again. "Ah, that's right. There is one thing I should tell you."

"What, is that?" asked Nova with a tilt of her head.

"The New Order has been acting strangely of late. Apparently, there are even quite a few hotheaded folks gathering in the Secession Sect. I doubt that even they would do anything extreme, but if you run into them, you would do well to go the other way."

"All right."

The man departed. Watching him go, Yuui asked, "Who was that?"

"I don't, know."

"Hmm?"

"Just a priest, who often comes to the Academy church. I don't even know, his name."

"Oh, I see…"

They decided to leave immediately and headed toward the station.

Leirest was a city in the north. It was some distance from the capital, but the Kusa Zuf road spanned the entire journey between them, making traveling fairly easy. The trade route was valuable to the kingdom, so there was always traffic in both directions. Many carriages frequented the road as well.

Layumatah was covering their travel expenses, so the three boarded a high-end carriage. They were the only passengers. Although it shook and jumped a lot because it ran at high speeds, transports of this quality were built to reduce that, so it ended up being just about as comfortable as a ride in the standard, slower models. On top of that, they didn't have to wait at the city gates. All it took was a flash of their travel permits, and they were able to pass through.

After discussing the situation for a bit, Ix quickly brought up Mali.

"She's the head of the Leirest Library. You met her, too, didn't you?" he asked Yuui.

"Yes, she gave me the book that one time..." she nodded from beneath her hood. "I wonder. She didn't very well seem like the kind of person to be involved in some plot."

"Yeah, I thought that, too." Ix recalled the face of the elderly white-haired lady. "Anyway, did you hear from Layumatah? About the, uh..."

"Witch? I did, but I still have no clue what they really are. I did my own investigations, but I was unable to find the term *witch* or anything resembling it in Central Standard, Kingdom Classical, or any of the languages I was able to look into at the Academy."

"You've had a lot of time, then," noted Ix in surprise. "When exactly did Layumatah ask you to look into this?"

"Actually, I was originally investigating witches in relation to a different incident. Layumatah contacted me because she'd learned about my research. It's sheer coincidence that you're who she wanted me to help... Though I suppose in one way it isn't exactly coincidence."

"And that is?"

"It's a long story, but... Uh, Ix, do you remember the adventurers who attacked you over the summer?"

"...Mm-hmm."

During an errand at the Adventurers' Guild, Ix had pointed out that some magic beast materials a pair of men were trying to turn in looked fake. The two adventurers later assaulted him in retribution. Fortunately, help came during the attack, and the ruffians were dumb enough to drop the magic beast materials in their rush to flee the scene.

"Those two were arrested. In the capital," said Yuui.

"Hmm? Huh, is that so," said Ix.

"It did not have anything to do with beating you up, though. They were actually booked for squatting in a public building. But something was off about them after they got arrested. It became clear after listening to them that they were the two who attacked you, which is when I asked them to go over the situation in detail," explained Yuui. The string of events seemed plausible enough to Ix.

She continued. "When I inquired about it, they said they did it *'because the witch made them.'*"

"Huh?" He let out a sound of confusion at the unexpected turn in the story.

"She'd threatened them, apparently. The adventurers believed the witch would capture them and do something terrible because they failed, so they fled all the way to the capital. Both looked like they hadn't eaten in ages and were jumping at every little sound. It truly did not appear to be an act."

"So they assaulted me because someone put them up to it?"

"No, that obviously comes down to them having to hand over the enedo teeth to the Guild," said Yuui with a deprecating smile. "And since you were the one who caused that to happen, they lashed out, since they were panicking over not being able to fulfill the witch's order."

"How bothersome..."

"I didn't feel any need to punish them further, so I just handed them over to the authorities. Did you want revenge, Ix?"

"No, I don't really care. I got more than enough money from those teeth anyway...," he responded, and then his eyebrows wrinkled. "With the way you're talking, it sounds like you're the one who captured them?"

"Ah..." Yuui quickly covered her mouth with her hand. "Uh... Well, yes, I was. Then I questioned them until the authorities arrived."

Just as Ix was thinking what an incredible coincidence that was, Nova, who hadn't said a peep so far, quickly opened her mouth and added, "Yuui saved me, too."

"N-Nova, no way, I didn't..."

"She saved you?" asked Ix, ignoring Yuui's attempt to stop the conversation.

"Yes. I was at a stall, in the capital, and I was being yelled at. Yuui happened to be nearby, and stepped in. She hid her face, but I realized, I'd heard the voice at the Academy. Then, we became friends. Thank you, Yuui."

"N-no, don't worry about it at all," replied the other girl.

"Yuui, you've always—"

"Ah, don't you think that's enough of that?" said Yuui, waving her hand and interrupting Nova. "Anyway, Nova, did you know Layumatah somehow before? How did she wind up selecting you for this job?"

"She, knows my family. Long ago, she helped with my wand. I told her, if she ever needed anything, to ask. She most likely asked me to help, because Lady Mali is a noble."

"...Wait," said Yuui as she pressed her hands to her cheeks. "It may be rude of me to inquire about this after being acquainted with you for this long, but are you from an aristocratic family?"

"Yes," replied Nova with her usual lifeless tone.

"O-oh, I see."

"But, they aren't that high in rank, so, please pay that no heed. Treat me the same, as always."

"Even if you say that..."

Ix turned away from Nova and Yuui, the former speaking in monotone and the latter's face cycling through a range of expressions, and turned his eyes out the window to the dimly lit surroundings. The same cloud-covered sky that hung over the capital extended far beyond it as well. The wind seemed strong, too, going off the swaying trees along the side of the road.

Their carriage passed smoothly by carts piled full of straw and people carrying heavy baggage on their backs. At this rate, they would be able to reach the station they were aiming for today before it started to rain.

Ix turned his eyes back inside the carriage, then spoke up. "Speaking of."

"Hmm?" Yuui turned to him.

"Those two adventurers who the witch threatened, where did they meet her?"

"Ah, yes, I had that question as well."

"Things'll be a lot faster if it happened to be at the library."

"It was in a village, actually."

"A village? So not in Leirest?"

"It is apparently close by. A town called Notswoll."

"Notswoll…?"

"Do you know it?"

"No… But I do feel like I've come across the name before." Ix blinked a few times. "Where was it…? I'm sure I've heard it somewhere."

Though the name stirred something in the depths of his memory, nothing surfaced. He hemmed and hawed for a while, but that only furthered his frustration over the memory, which seemed so close, yet so far.

Yuui watched him struggle and tried to lend a helping hand.

"Well, if this village is near Leirest, then we should be able to research from the city, right?"

"Yeah, that's true, but…" Ix leaned his head on his fist.

"Um, Nova, do you know anything of Notswoll?" asked Yuui.

"No."

Obviously, there was no way they would have been fortunate enough to get a *yes*.

3

Having arrived in Leirest, Yuui gazed outside with scrutiny.

Though she'd last visited this summer, the streets somehow looked different. If she had to describe the scene in the common tongue, she would likely call it *restless*. Even the people who were just passing through seemed giddy, like they were floating on air.

And it wasn't just the pedestrians, either. The facades of the buildings lining the streets were covered in vibrant decorations. Beside the roads, people were setting up wooden figures. Leirest was always bustling—it was a merchant town, after all—but that was nothing compared to this fervor.

"It's the festival," remarked Ix when he saw Yuui staring.

"Festival?"

"The Feast of Meat. The harvest festival. They do it in the capital, don't they—?"

"An event to give thanks to God, for the year's harvest," interjected Nova abruptly. "The greater the celebration, the greater the thanks, to God. Each town celebrates differently, with instruments, singing, parades. Based on this year's calendar, the festival, will be in three days."

"Oh, now that you mention it..."

Yuui did remember something happening around this time the year before. Back then, she'd shut herself up in her room, but she did recall the obnoxious noise from the celebration. It had been so loud, she couldn't fall asleep that night.

So that was the harvest festival...

Lukutta also held an event celebrating the harvest, but it was a solemn ceremony where you couldn't even let out a cough.

Ix continued the explanation.

"That's what they say it's for, anyway, but it's really just a huge banquet. People eat meat, drink alcohol, and generally party all night long. A lot of couples get together at the Feast of Meat, too, so—"

"Ah, I think I get the gist." Yuui sighed. "You mean to say it is the kind of thing that would raise eyebrows in the New Order."

The New Order was a Marayist denomination. Unlike the Old Order, which was predominant in the kingdom, the New Order criticized the government's authoritarianism and insisted that each person's individual labor reflected the will of God.

"I wonder... I feel like both Old Order and New Order would accept its practical significance."

"Don't they just want to let off some steam?"

"Sure, they want to have fun, too, but there's also a seasonal problem." Ix shrugged. "You dealt with it last year, right? The sky's almost always clouded over during winter in the kingdom. We barely get any sun. And if it snows, it's hard to travel. So if everyone has as much fun as they want, it helps them get ready for enduring the winter."

"Have you ever taken part in the festival?" asked Yuui.

"No," replied Ix quickly.

"…Thought so."

The carriage station sat on the edge of the city, both for convenience and so the stench wouldn't be too overwhelming. From there, they headed into the center of town, into an area with rows of shops and homes for the wealthy. The library was nearby.

Partway through, however, Nova halted.

"What's wrong?" asked Yuui, turning back after she'd passed her by a few steps.

"May we, go separate ways, for now?" requested Nova quietly. "I want to, look into something."

"Uh…but weren't you brought on to make sure things went smoothly with Mali, since she's a noble like you?"

"If she's the head librarian, you should be able to meet her, by going to the library. And earlier, you both said, that you had met her."

"Where are you going? And what are you looking into?" asked Ix.

"To research Notswoll, at the church. Yuui's target, is there. I think it may be necessary, later. They should be more, accommodating, to a noble."

"I suppose that's true…," said Yuui.

"You know where it is?" asked Ix.

"No," replied Nova.

He gave her a general lay of the land, and they agreed on a place to meet back up. Nova gave a short good-bye and left. Her small form was quickly swallowed by the crowd.

The two continued walking, and Ix tilted his head.

"How long's Nova been following you around?"

"Only since just recently. We met near the end of break." At the beginning of summer, Yuui had become estranged from the friends she'd had until that point, but then Nova came along, almost as if to fill the hole her previous acquaintances had left. "I had seen her at the lectures beforehand, but we didn't start speaking until that incident. Also, asking *'how long she's been following me around'* makes it sounds like she is stalking me or something, Ix."

"So you saved her, huh? You're okay with the adventuring thing, then? Seems doing that work in the capital got you dragged into some dangerous stuff."

"I wouldn't say I was dragged into anything..."

"Just be careful. That wand's powerful, but it's also fragile."

"To be honest, I would say that occurrence was the wand's fault."

"I don't follow."

"I'm phrasing it so you won't understand."

"What the...?" Ix's expression turned serious as he looked at her in confusion.

In reality, Yuui had gotten involved in more than just the two incidents she'd informed Ix about. Ever since going back to the capital, she'd taken to roaming around the city every once in a while, getting herself wrapped up in whatever perilous situations she could find.

All of that was her attempt to live up to the wand that her father had bequeathed to her. It had an incredibly moral disposition, so it was impossible to use unless you possessed a just heart. After considering what kind of person was suited to that sort of wand, she'd found herself acting like a hero of late.

"I don't get that Nova at all," remarked Ix. "She's gotten involved with someone from the east despite being kingdom nobility. And she was so grateful you helped her..."

"Hmm, I wonder...," started Yuui before faltering. "If I had to say, I think..."

"What?"

"Oh, nothing. It's only speculation, so I shouldn't say anything."

The route to the library was a familiar one for these two, so they arrived without getting lost. The building had been constructed at a time when city libraries were considered fashionable, so its exterior was richly decorated. By contrast, half the texts lining the shelves inside were randomly gathered documents and bundles of paper.

The library was quiet both inside and out, the fervor of the festival seemingly unable to penetrate its tranquility. Then again, there weren't many who used it in the first place. The building's particular scent assailed them as they entered, spurring Yuui to remember her many trips here over the summer, where she'd bury herself in books.

They went straight in toward a cordoned-off area, where they found a man sitting, his eyes drooping half closed.

"Ix, do you mind keeping quiet?" Yuui asked before they approached.

"Why—?"

"Because." She held him back, then stepped forward. "Excuse me, may I have a moment of your time?"

"H-huh?" The man raised his head in surprise. Perhaps people didn't often speak to him. He looked at Yuui, hood pulled down over her face, before his eyes continued to Ix, behind her.

"We would like to meet with the head librarian, if possible...," said Yuui.

"Oh, uh, and who are you?" asked the man.

"Oh, excuse me." She took her student ID from her pocket and placed it on the desk.

"A student..." The man squinted as he stared at the ID, then blinked. "For the head librarian?"

"Yes."

"That would be me."

"…What?"

"…Huh?"

For a moment, Yuui just stared at the man's blank face. She was likely making the same expression.

The man had short white hair. His eyes were small, and his hunched shoulders made him appear old. Since he was working in the library, he must have been a noble, but everything about him, from his clothes to his manner of speaking, all appeared rather humble. To put it bluntly, he seemed poor.

"Um, well…," started the man, his eyes roving.

"Oh, m-my apologies," said Yuui with a bow. "I could have sworn the head librarian was an elderly lady…"

"A-ah." He gave an exaggerated nod. "Her. Yeah, she retired recently. Now I'm the head. That lady was my aunt."

"And now she's…?"

"I'd been telling her for ages that she wasn't getting any younger and should think about retiring. And eventually, her health really did catch up to her. Everyone had to practically force her out, you know."

"You don't mean—"

"Oh, no. She's alive." The man gave a weak smile. "But she's not in great shape. Though she still pops in randomly, so I can't really relax too much…"

"Just to confirm, Mali was the name, yes?" she asked.

"Uh, mine?"

"Your aunt's."

"Oh, yeah, yes. That's right. So it was her you wanted to talk to?"

"Yes, it was. Would it be possible to meet with her?"

"Uh, I'm not really sure…" He crossed his arms and stared up at the ceiling. "You could ask, but I think it'd be hard for anyone to meet her who isn't a relative… Probably…depends on what you want to discuss with her. Uh, what was it you want to talk about anyway? I could try asking for you."

"It's about the work she did on the wand wall. There is

something odd about her repairs from a technical perspective, which I want to inquire about. That's from about sixty years back, though."

"Sixty whole years?" the man cried. "Ah, sorry. Work on the wand wall, huh...? I've never heard anything about that. Did it come up in your studies at the Academy or something?"

"You could say that."

"Hmm. Well, I'll try telling her..."

"I would appreciate it."

It was raining when they left, the kind of fine mist that dampened the air, to which no kingdom citizen paid any mind. The pair walked in silence.

Ix looked sullen and wasn't speaking up, so Yuui went first.

"...I feel like we've suddenly run into a dead end."

"Yeah." Ix's mouth was hidden behind his hand. "But if Mali's in bad shape and stuck in her manor, she probably didn't have anything to do with the wand wall being undone..."

"If she has no connection, that's all well and good." Yuui held her hands palm up. "But thanks to what we just heard, the witch thing does seem to be just a rumor. At the very least, I do not believe immortal people retire from poor health."

"...That was obvious from the start."

"You think so? I hadn't ruled out the possibility."

"An immortal? That's just cra—"

"Dragons existed."

When Yuui said that, Ix looked down and shut his mouth.

Dragons. Beings with infinite magic who'd bestowed humanity with countless gifts; massive creatures who'd gone extinct more than a thousand years ago. There were legends about them in every region of the world. The "dragon magic" they'd wielded had become a kind of catchall; it referred to varieties of all-powerful magic that humans were incapable of using.

Ix and Yuui had met one of those legendary creatures. The dragon, who had waited for more than a millennium to converse with a human, granted the two of them one of its hearts before fading from existence, bringing its species to a close. Just because something was a folktale or a legend didn't mean it could be taken lightly. Ix of all people should understand that.

They couldn't yet be certain that tales of immortality, cannibalism, or undoing the wand wall were beyond the realm of possibility. If those were components of witch lore, then they were worth investigating.

After all, researching every possible avenue was what had led them to their encounter with a dragon.

They had agreed to meet up with Nova in a square on the eastern side of the city. Preparations for the festival were going on here as well, and plenty of young people were in high spirits. On the opposite side of the square was an official who seemed to be policing the area with a sharp eye. His presence clearly signaled that he would arrest anyone who went too far.

The pair quickly found Nova, hedged in on either side by tall people and looking rather squished.

"Ah, Nova," called out Yuui with a wave as she went over. "Did we keep you waiting? You seem to have finished quicker than we did."

"No, I just found him," replied the girl with a shrug.

"Found who?"

"Me."

Yuui's vision was suddenly filled with black. For a moment, she couldn't understand what was going on. After taking a few steps back, she finally laid eyes on a man's face. It soon dawned on her that this fellow, clad in all black, had stepped between her and Nova.

He was thin and middle-aged. His features were strong and chiseled, but his cheeks were puffy, and there was little life in his eyes. He had a stubbly beard and shaggy hair, which made him look even more suspicious at the moment, what with them drenched from the rain. But he was wearing black clerical vestments. That meant he was a member of the Marayist clergy, but he didn't look the part at all. Visually, he had more in common with a beggar on the street.

"Hiya," he greeted, raising a hand.

"And you are…?" asked Yuui.

"Gidens." He held out his hand. "I'm the reader in Notswoll. How'd you folks hear about that anyway?"

"Hear about what?"

Gidens chuckled at Yuui's confusion and said, "'Bout the witch."

4

"Well, if this ain't a hovel," muttered Gidens after one look at the shop. "This really the place?"

Ix didn't answer as he opened the door. There was no one in the front section of the store.

"Morna?" called Ix toward the back. A rattling came in response. She was in here somewhere, apparently.

This shop belonged to Morna, who had also studied under Munzil. Currently, Ix was living and working here as her apprentice.

He pushed his way into the place, past haphazard piles of crafting materials, plus wands and staffs lined up neatly on display. As he moved farther in, the inner door opened violently.

"I-Ixie."

There stood—or perhaps it was more appropriate to say, there wobbled—an incredibly unhealthy-looking woman in a half crouch. Her skin was sickly pale, and her height was reduced from her slouched posture. Long, damaged hair clung to her waist, and her patchwork clothing was utterly filthy. There was certainly only one person like this in the entire kingdom.

"H-hee-hee-hee, I-Ixieee… Gurgh!"

She let out a disturbing sound as she approached Ix, who

quickly pushed her head down with his hand. The feel of her dry hair seemed to linger on his palm even after he removed it.

Face devoid of expression, he inquired, "Where's Ottou?"

"F-f-f-for some reason, he hasn't come in the past couple of days… S-so…"

"You've been shut in the shop this whole time, haven't you?"

"Y-yeah. W-welcome back."

He pointed behind himself wordlessly.

"Wh-what…?" asked Morna as she peered outside. Her face turned pale. She pressed a hand over her mouth. "Urgh…"

"Don't puke here—it'd be a pain to clean up," said Ix as he supported her and led her toward the back. He turned back to say, "Just come on in. Seems meeting two new people at once was too much for her."

They needed a place to talk, so everyone ended up coming into the shop; Yuui, Nova, and Gidens were all there. Ix was aware of how bad Morna was with people, but it didn't often cause her to throw up. It must have been so bad this time around since she'd gone without contact for the past few days.

Ix patted Morna's bony back while he cast his eyes about the back room. It was far worse in here than when he'd left to go to the capital. She hadn't been taking care of the cleaning, or feeding herself, for that matter. Couldn't really be helped with Ottou gone, though…

Once he was sure Morna had calmed down, Ix returned to the front room of the shop. This section was a mess, too, but considering there were actually places to stand, it was better than the back.

"Is Morna all right?" asked Yuui, concerned.

"Yeah, she's fine. She'll bounce back with a bit of rest."

As he looked around, he noticed Nova had crouched down in the corner of the room. Her hands were on her knees, and she wasn't moving at all. It was almost like she was saying, "My job's done here."

"Ah, all good now?" asked Gidens, tearing his eyes from the

row of wands and staffs to look at Ix. "I can't tell a good wand from a bad one, but did that tall lady from before make all these?"

"Yeah," replied Ix.

"Huh… How 'bout the ones you made?"

"How'd you know I was a wandmaker?"

"You shook my hand," said Gidens like it was obvious, and he opened his right hand. "You got calluses in all sorts of weird places. It's clear as day that's the palm of a craftsman, 'cause all you do is use weird tools. But, oh boy, I never thought a run-down little wand shop like this could exist. Sure you ain't just overcharging for a couple of nice sticks you found? …Nah, I'm just messing." He placed a hand on Ix's shoulder. "Sorry, I got a friend who worked hard to save up but still couldn't buy one in the end. Couldn't help that little jab slipping out."

"…You're Notswoll's priest, aren't you?" asked Ix as he looked at Gidens suspiciously.

"I never said I was a priest; I'm just a reader. A reader goes round all the little villages that don't got churches, and they recite scriptures and hymns and whatnot to folks. Some other person is Notswoll's official priest. Not that I've met them, though."

Ix brought his hand to his chin and stared at Gidens.

"Hey now, don't look at me like that," the man replied. "You've got things you want to ask me, right? I need to leave town the day after tomorrow, so if you have questions, hurry up and get on them."

"Where are you going?" asked Yuui.

"Not just going, going back. To Notswoll. I got to be there for the Feast of Meat. I just came to Leirest to help Gramps with some things. Buying stuff for the festival. But I been traveling round the villages, so they started to miss me *here*…" Gidens chattered on. "Ah, you don't want to hear 'bout me, do you? Anyway, I went to visit the church, and that young lady grabbed ahold of me."

Nova gave only a small nod when Gidens gestured at her. He shook his head, resigned that she really wasn't going to speak, then turned back toward Yuui and Ix.

"So where exactly did you folks hear about the witch?"

"W-wait," interjected Yuui as she waved her hand side to side. "Do you mean to say that you know of the witch? Are they in Notswoll?"

"…I asked first now, didn't I?" said Gidens as he flashed his teeth in a smile. "But it's fine. Yeah, I sure do, miss. The witch lives in the forest by Notswoll."

The quick response made Ix and Yuui exchange glances. Gidens looked back at them, still grinning.

After a few seconds of silence, Ix slowly inquired, "Have you seen the, uh…witch?"

"Of course. Not just me, either; all the villagers have seen her at least once. That's 'cause she comes the night of the Feast of Meat every year."

"Huh?"

"What?"

Both Ix and Yuui let out cries of surprise at the same time.

"All right, I turned a blind eye to your lack of manners twice now. Next you're going to answer my question." Gidens glared at the two. "Right, so everyone in the village knows about the witch, but none of them would tell an outsider. So how was it that you folks heard about this?"

They didn't mention the issue with the wand wall, but they did tell Gidens about the two adventurers Yuui had captured in the capital.

Once their story was finished, Gidens crossed his arms and muttered to himself. He mulled something over for a time, frowning.

"Sorry to say, but I don't know anything 'bout these adventurers. I don't even know what the witch does normally. There's not much I can tell you."

"How about this. Do enedo live in the woods?" asked Yuui with a finger raised.

"Who knows. People don't tread there, so I can't really say what do or don't live there…"

"People don't go into the woods?" asked Ix with a furrowed brow.

Forests were a treasure trove of natural resources. They were particularly valuable within the kingdom, to the point where it wasn't too uncommon for battles to be fought over them. The situation would be different if magic beasts dwelled there, but the fact that there was a village nearby meant there shouldn't have been any dangerous creatures. People should have been swarming into the area by now.

"I mean, they do go in a little. Folks need firewood. But there aren't many curious enough to go too— Ah," responded Gidens when he seemed to realize something and smiled. "That's right. You might not have heard that part."

"Heard what part?" asked Yuui.

"I said she comes on the night of the Feast of Meat, yeah? But that's not 'cause she wants to dance with the villagers. It's a harvest festival for her, too."

"You mean—"

"She comes to gobble people up. Just like we feast on meat and drink spirits, the witch devours human beings. When she shows up, it's the end of the festival. Everybody and their grandma shuts themselves in their homes and does everything to protect their little ones so they don't get carried off. The witch can't find you if you're in a house, see. *That's* the kind of terror lurking in the forest. It's also why no one gets too close or talks about it to outsiders. They don't want to be found out."

"……"

Not knowing what to say, Ix closed his mouth, which had been hanging open. Yuui was likely in a similar state of disbelief.

"You two look like the cat's got your tongue," noticed Gidens, accurately, as he glanced between them. "So that's the witch for you. She's not just some powerful magic user."

"…Has anyone ever actually been eaten? Like, people don't just say that?" asked Ix.

"Ha-ha, I thought the same as you before, so I did a little reading up on it. When I did, I found some actual records of it in the church." Gidens's smile still didn't fade as he spoke. "Yeah, they were definitely eaten. That, or at the very least, people have gone missing on the day of the festival under '*unusual circumstances*.' It's not just some folktale about ancient history, either. The last time someone got devoured was twenty years back. I didn't see it with my own eyes, however, 'cause I was only sent out there eighteen years ago. Everyone in town remembers it, though. A little baby got devoured the night of the festival."

"An infant?"

"That's what the records say. Guess they were swallowed before anyone had even named them." Gidens shrugged at the horror of the story. "This happened not long after the baby was born. Their mother was ill and died during childbirth..."

"Ill? What about the father?"

"If memory serves...he wasn't there in the first place."

"Uh-huh..." Suddenly, Ix glanced away and put a hand over his mouth. He took a slow, deep breath. "...And what had the mother come down with?"

"Huh? Don't know off the top of my head. Is that an important detail?"

"No, it's just...that was when sonim was going around."

"Hmm...? Ah... Yeah, that was it. Now that you mention it, it's coming back to me. Yeah, the mother did have sonim. I remember reading that." Gidens nodded until he seemed caught by surprise and stopped in confusion. "Hold on. That's strange, isn't it? I haven't heard of a child being born alive to a mother with sonim..."

Suddenly, the strength left Ix's legs, and he collapsed into a chair close by. Then he stared up at the ceiling, an expression of shock on his face.

Did that mean...?

Could it be...?

"I-Ix, are you all right?" asked Yuui, looking concerned as she stood in front of him. She'd also caught on, he realized. Glancing around, he noticed that Gidens and Nova, too, were staring at him.

"Yeah...," he replied dimly. "Do you...remember anything about before that?"

"Huh?" asked Gidens with a confused expression.

"Do you recall anything about the people who were gobbled up before that baby?"

"Oh, uh, there was...that's right, a young girl."

"A girl?"

"It's coming back to me slowly. There was a very young girl. She was devoured on the day of a storm. That must have been about eighty years ago. And before that—"

"Eighty years?" Ix held up a hand to stop the reader. "I can't believe this—are you about to tell us that the witch is immortal?"

"What, you know 'bout that, too?"

5

When he saw the sun dip in the sky, Gidens left the shop.

Yuui returned from going out to buy dinner, and Morna had come to the front of the shop, finally recovered. She seemed to be chatting with Ix about something. Nova, on the other hand, was silent as usual, still crouching in the exact same place as she'd been when Yuui left.

"H-hee-hee, Layumatah...the wand wall...," cried Morna excitedly when she heard about their fellow apprentice. "H-hoo-hoo-hwee, a-a-amazing. I want to see."

"I thought you would say that...," said Ix with a sigh. "But we've hit a snag straight from the get-go. We can't meet Mali, and the witch seems completely unrelated, but if we report to Layumatah with what we have now..."

"Will she be angry?" asked Yuui.

"She'll make us do it over. We'll have to keep at it until we get the results she wants."

"I see…"

Yuui had met Layumatah a couple of times, but she'd been so overwhelmed by the mask and clothing that she hadn't gotten a read on the woman at all. Yuui knew she was strange, not to be outdone by Ix or Morna in that respect, but she'd expected as much the moment she heard Layumatah was Munzil's first apprentice.

As the four of them tucked into dinner, the conversation naturally turned to the witch.

"She eats people; she's immortal… It all seems to fit perfectly," remarked Ix with his arms crossed.

"M-M-Master said th-those things?" asked Morna in confusion. "I've n-never heard that before."

"Layumatah said she only heard about it from him once. She hadn't ruled out the possibility that he was just making up crap."

"But according to Gidens, the witch does exist," countered Yuui.

"There's still room for doubt, though. We don't know if we can trust what he says…"

"At the very least, you have to accept that there's a legend about the witch in Notswoll," she insisted.

"…Oh yeah," said Ix, realizing something. "Morna, you ever heard of a town called Notswoll?"

"H-huh? N-no, I haven't…"

"Oh… Then maybe it doesn't have anything to do with wand-making…" He crossed his arms again. "Could it really be…?"

Yuui knew what was on his mind.

Ix was wondering if the baby the witch had eaten twenty years ago was actually *him*. Ix had been abandoned as an infant outside Munzil's shop. No one knew anything about his parents or his history. But the child in the story fit the timing of when he was found, and the fact that the mother had come down with sonim made it all the more likely.

Normally, infected women would birth stillborn children. The odds a baby could survive that were almost infinitesimal—only one instance had been recorded in the entire kingdom. The child who'd survived lacked mana, something that every single human being possessed. Ix was also a human born without mana, so it stood to reason that his mother had caught sonim.

If he was truly that baby from Notswoll, it raised a number of questions.

"By the way," spoke up Nova unexpectedly as she raised her hand.

"Ah!" Morna froze.

"Sorry," Nova replied.

"Ah, h-h-ho, oh, no..." The wandmaker worked furiously to get the words out, her expression tense.

"You don't have to respond to Morna every time she gets like this. Otherwise, this'll never end," remarked Ix coldly. "Anyway, what's up?"

"It's just, something's, bothering me," said Nova falteringly. "Is immortality, possible?"

Just like that, they were instantly thrust into the topic they'd been dancing around. The three of them shut their mouths. But if they were going to investigate the witch, they would need to actually consider it.

"Is that within the realms of standard magicology or are we including dragon magic as well?" asked Yuui, trying to determine whether they were presupposing finite or infinite mana.

"Either," replied Nova.

After a moment of silence, with everyone attempting to gauge the other's next statement, Ix wound up the first to speak.

"I don't think it's possible. Of course, that's only based on the knowledge that I have available to me now."

"Let's hear your reasoning," insisted Yuui.

"Calling it 'reasoning' is giving me too much credit. Anyway, it's simple. There aren't any immortal creatures around. Not that we know of anyway. Right?" He glanced at each of their faces.

"So that would mean the witch is the sole exception to that rule. Which seems hard to believe. Don't you think that's just the, uh, common-sense conclusion? Guess that's not about how it would work or not, though, just about whether they exist."

Yuui nodded once. "It is a simplistic train of thought, but I think it is an appropriate conclusion within the field of standard magicology," she responded. "However, it is not the conclusion one would come to if they were considering special magicology. There are no immortal creatures in this world, but all living creatures have finite mana. What would happen, however, if the witch had infinite mana? I'm sure you are aware, but the elves' long life span is often attributed to their greater mana volume."

"The connection between life span and mana is an unfounded wives' tale," interjected Ix with a shake of his head. "Mana is just a power source. It has no effect on the world in and of itself. Not unless it's converted using a wand."

While Yuui did largely accept what he said, she felt this topic deserved further debate. She thought a moment.

"That's not necessarily true," she insisted. "There is a general trend of long life among famous magic users. While we cannot be certain this is a causal link, we can clearly see a correlation. If that's the case, could there perhaps be some connection that we just don't currently understand? This is also not about how it would work or not work, though, just about its existence."

"Way to turn my words against me."

"Well, both what you and I came up with now is only a potentiality."

"We going to talk about realities, too, not just potentialities? A bigger issue would be whether infinite magic is even possible or not..."

"What about drawing mana from nearby organisms?" mused Yuui, thinking of the dragon. "It could be similar to immortality. You could use a spell to convert mana into some sort of energy to increase your life span."

"No spell like that exists at the moment, not even in our wildest dreams."

"I have heard that ancient forest sages used incantations that we are still unable to fully explain. Perhaps the witch possesses similar expertise?"

"Forest sage magic is unexplainable because of the natural wands they used. There is something fascinating about ancient wisdom surpassing modern knowledge," conceded Ix with a nod. "But even so. Modern magicology was built up slowly over a huge span of time by hundreds of people. I might be able to accept someone being ahead of current advancements by ten or twenty years, but it seems too improbable to me that someone could possibly be hundreds of years ahead of the curve."

"Hmm..."

Their back-and-forth ground to a halt. The two of them fell to thinking, and Morna shakily raised her hand.

Yuui's eyes widened, and she asked, "Morna?"

"A-a-ah, this might be backtracking a bit, but, um..."

"What is it?"

"H-how do you c-c-confirm something is immortal?"

Basic though her point was, it was also on the nose.

That is true..., thought Yuui as she cast her eyes down.

No matter how much they debated the possibility of immortality, there was no way to actually confirm their theories.

According to Gidens, the kingdom first started keeping land surveillance records of its territory about six hundred years ago. At that time, something that resembled the witch was already living near Notswoll. The records from back then weren't about the witch herself, but rather about certain occurrences involving her. In other words, they were accounts of people disappearing from town under "*unusual circumstances.*"

All those documents proved was that the witch had lived some six hundred years ago, nothing more. That was a life span far beyond what would normally be expected, but it wasn't immortality.

In the end, even if an eternal creature existed, there would be no way to prove their immortality without another undying being to measure their life span. They could discuss it all they wanted, but they would never move beyond a theory.

If they could come up with a hypothesis as to how immortality could be possible, then they could at least consider if it would be sustainable. At this point, however, they weren't capable of getting that far. Considering they didn't even know why creatures died in the first place, it wasn't surprising they'd gotten stuck.

Morna's mumblings had broken the atmosphere of debate. Besides, if the witch did exist, they could simply get the answer straight from the horse's mouth on the day of the festival. Assuming they didn't get gobbled up, of course…

"Thank you," said Nova. Thus, the discussion drew to a close with no conclusion reached.

Outside, it had already grown dark. Ix would be staying in the shop, of course, but Yuui and Nova would also be spending the night, so they made a space for them to sleep. There were no guest rooms, so the two of them ended up sharing a room.

"Thank you for today," said Yuui with a bow once they were alone.

"For, what?" asked Nova.

"For finding Gidens. We've made great progress on investigating the witch because of that. Even if Ix seems unsatisfied."

"About, Mali?"

"We'll think about her again tomorrow. Though our only real course of action is to pray our message reaches her and she agrees to meet…"

Yuui glanced sideways at Nova, who was nodding in agreement.

Her bangs always hid half her face, and her peculiar way of speaking and flat affect made her very difficult to read, in a different way from Ix. She always seemed exactly the same. It made Yuui wonder if the girl had emotions or was even thinking at all.

The witch…

Yuui lay in bed, pondering things vaguely.

Ix seemed to doubt her existence, but Yuui thought it was likely the witch did exist.

That wasn't because she believed what Gidens or those two adventurers had to say.

The proof was the woods.

If there was a forest by Notswoll, would people really be able to resist it? No magic beasts were confirmed to live there, and its location near Leirest made it ideal. If such a forest existed, it should have been chopped down long ago. Her own country had been invaded by the kingdom, which was why she well knew that its people loved to destroy woodlands the moment they found them to convert them into farms. Or perhaps they destroyed them because of Marayist teachings. The kingdom wanted the resources and land to make food, of course, but the deeper reason was that its culture placed no emphasis on living together with nature. Its people believed that everything was a gift given to them by their god, and so they had the right to use it as they saw fit. It was the exact opposite of what the Lukutta believed, which was that since everything was a gift given to them by their god, they should use it carefully. Yuui couldn't help feeling curious as to why even that would be different between their cultures.

But that was why Yuui thought it was so strange that this convenient forest still existed. There had to be some reason for that. Such as if something terrifying dwelled in those woods.

At this point, Nova, who Yuui had thought was already asleep, murmured to her.

"...Yuui?"

"Y-yes?"

"What is it like, living in the kingdom?"

"I'm not sure what to say..."

"Do you want to go back, to Lukutta?"

Yuui wasn't able to answer that question immediately. Instead, she said, "Why do you ask...?"

"No real reason."

"......"

This was the first time Nova had brought up something like this. Her face was turned toward Yuui, but it was dark, so Yuui couldn't make out her expression.

After a short moment of silence, Yuui said, "To be honest... I'm not entirely sure myself." Amid the darkness, her words didn't seem to lead anywhere, as though they were floating above her head as she spoke to herself. "I appreciate what you've done for me, Nova, but I can't say living in the kingdom is pleasant. There is no place for easterners in this country. But...there is also no place for me back in Lukutta. I have lost my family, my friends, the village I was born in. Lukutta may be my homeland, but it is no longer my home. There would be nothing I could do if I went back..."

"Aren't you from, a lineage respected there?"

"That's all there is to it," said Yuui with a pained smile. "Unless I were sent to be queen?"

"Is that, so?" Nova replied curtly before she trailed off. However, not much later she said, "Continuing, the discussion..."

"About my future?"

"From, dinner. Ix said, there were no immortal beings."

"Hmm? Oh yes, he did."

"And it made me think, of a lecture from before. It was, years ago, so you wouldn't know."

"What did the lecture talk about?"

"The fact that, immortal creatures, exist."

"Huh? Where?"

"Everywhere."

1

Ix looked around, marveling that a place like this in Leirest even existed.

Massive houses lined either side of the wide road. Perhaps *houses* wasn't the right word for them. *Mansions*, that was better. The buildings were set far apart, with trees and hedges growing on their gardens to block the view from one building to the next. Despite the morning hour, the street was almost devoid of pedestrians. Ix couldn't see any people in the mansions, either, which made him feel like he was the only person there.

This was different from both the heart of the city and its outskirts. It was silent.

Ix double-checked the address written on the envelope and wondered if he was really in the right place.

He'd been the only one to come here. It wasn't the kind of errand you sent multiple people on. Yuui and Nova were in the library checking the consistency of the tales on witches. Morna was holed up in the shop, as always.

The mansion he was headed toward was set back from the road at the end of a gently curving path. A mild breeze blew beneath the clouded sky, scattering leaves from the trees.

Motion caught Ix's eye. He squinted to find a woman who

appeared to be a gardener. She wore coveralls and was doing something around the grounds, too engrossed in her work to notice Ix.

As he stepped over dry, crinkly leaves, the mansion properly came into view. It was a two-story edifice made from reddish stone, but Ix couldn't tell how far back it extended. It was obviously massive.

The entrance seemed sturdy, and as he approached, he wondered how hard he'd have to knock for them to be able to hear inside, but the door opened on its own. Or rather, the man who opened it had just stuck his face out.

"I'm—" started Ix, before he was interrupted.

"Yes, very good, sir. Please do come in," said the man with a bow.

A servant, perhaps? His outfit was almost entirely black, and he even wore gloves of the same color to match. He had pale blond hair that was parted evenly down the center, and his age wasn't clear from his face. His straight, rigid posture resembled that of a statue.

Upon doing as the man asked and stepping inside, Ix was immediately overwhelmed.

He couldn't fathom why the building would need to be this spacious or extravagantly decorated. It was like an even more dazzling version of Layamutah's shop. Every single thing was elaborate, from the paintings on the walls to the candlesticks. Ix could only imagine they were all there to shock the mansion's visitors. That could very well have been the reason for its splendor.

Behind him, the door gave a quiet sound as it closed shut.

"Please follow me," bade the man as he gracefully walked off. "May I call you by your given name, Mr. Ix?"

"I don't have any other names you could call me by."

"Oh…is that so? How very rude of me."

"Anyway, how do you know who I am?" asked Ix, but the man only gave him a bow that seemed loaded with meaning.

They climbed the stairs and passed through a landing made of a single massive sheet of glass. Once on the second floor, Ix could feel a breeze from the outside. One side of the passageway lacked a wall. Beyond a railing, you could see down into a courtyard. The same type of passage ran on the left and right, as well as the far end. In other words, the mansion had been constructed in a square around the courtyard so that the interior opened onto it. This central garden was lined with flower beds, and servants were currently bustling back and forth to bring round tables into it. They were so focused on their work that they didn't notice the people watching them from above.

"We will be holding a gala here in the courtyard for a large number of guests," said the man. "We're planning it for this evening, actually, as a sort of pre-celebration for the Feast of Meat. Every year it's hosted at a different residence, and it offers an invaluable opportunity for the host to flaunt their status. We have been consumed with preparations the past few days."

"Won't matter if you can't hold it," remarked Ix.

He looked up at the rain clouds blanketing the sky. The air felt damp. It was the kind of weather that threatened to break into showers at any moment.

"There won't be any issues, so long as the rain is mild. We'll pass cloth across the second-floor balconies to fend it off if need be."

"You could just hold it inside."

"That would not be possible," clarified the man with a smile.

Ix was about to ask why it wouldn't, but before he could, the man opened a door and bade him to head that way.

Ix stepped into what looked like a parlor. He was no longer surprised at each and every display of luxury, but he did have a hard time feeling at ease here. They could stand to reduce the number of objects in this place. He took a seat at the behest of the man, who then asked him to wait a moment before leaving Ix alone in the room.

Ix took the envelope out of his inside pocket and twirled it in his hand. He was regretting not just handing it over at the door and leaving. Being here was uncomfortable.

A short while later, the same man returned. He poured tea

into a porcelain teacup that seemed as thin as a feather. Steam spiraled up into the air.

"I appreciate your hospitality," said Ix as he spread one arm, "but this isn't that important an errand. I just need to deliver this envelope."

"And to whom is it addressed?"

"I was told to give it to someone in charge of the Obryle family."

"May I see the contents?"

"Uh…" Ix thought for a moment. "I wasn't told to keep others from seeing it. I guess it won't hurt as long as it reaches the higher-ups."

"Then if you don't mind."

The man sat in the chair opposite Ix. He broke the seal and read the letter inside. There wasn't much written.

The Obryles were a clan of influential merchants based in Leirest. They dealt in a wide variety of goods and were involved in all sorts of transactions that took place across the city. Ix had heard that they'd hailed from outside the kingdom, but thanks to their influence skyrocketing during the sonim plague, their name carried weight across the entire nation. Their economic and political clout rivaled that of even higher-ranking aristocrats.

The only reason Ix had ended up in the home of such a prominent family was because of an order from Layumatah. Apparently, she'd purchased some materials she would need for making the new wand wall lock from the Obryles. Her request was asking a lot of them, so she'd made Ix hand deliver a letter expressing her gratitude.

"How very kind of her," noted the man with a smile when he finished reading. "Ms. Layumatah is a valuable customer. Just being able to continue doing business with her is thanks enough. Would you like a reply?"

"I don't think it matters. But should you be sending a reply before even showing it to someone in charge here?"

"That is not an issue." The man smiled and brought a hand to his chest. "My name is Elion. I am the fourth son of the Obryle family. I have a certain level of authority over our transactions."

"...You're Elion Obryle?"

"I am indeed."

"Uh-huh..."

"I apologize for misleading you."

"Are there any other members of your family here?"

"There is my father, who is the head of the household; my mother; and two of my brothers. I don't feel you would get along very well with them, so I have asked the servants to ensure you don't cross paths."

"I appreciate the concern."

"By the way, Mr. Ix, you earlier said that you have no other name by which I could address you," said Elion as he folded his hands and gazed at Ix. "But I was under the impression you were Munzil Alreff's adopted son."

"Oh... Yeah, legally speaking, that's true, but I was really just his apprentice. What about it?"

"I would have thought you'd taken his surname. Shouldn't your real name be Ix Alreff? It may not be by blood, but you are father and son."

"Ix Alreff...?" He couldn't help bringing his hand up to hide his mouth.

Now that he mentions it...that is how it works.

Children usually took their parents' surnames. Ix had never heard of a household where only the kids were without them. But he didn't have one. Even Master had told him he didn't have one, and that was how it was written on their family register. He'd never considered claiming the Alreff name for himself.

"Ah, my apologies if I've upset you," added Elion with an open arm when he saw Ix fall silent.

"It's fine..."

"Through my work, I have developed a bit of an interest in

names. It is the most crucial detail in trade, after all. Oftentimes, a single moniker can change the outcome of a deal."

"I would've thought a merchant wouldn't want the outcome of a deal to be influenced."

"Well, we do interact with nobles, and even if we didn't, we have to handle merchants who don't behave as they should." He gave a wry chuckle. "There are benefits, of course. For example, if you move from calling someone by their surname to calling them by their given name, you can play up a relationship of friendship. It's a way of currying favor."

"Really?" Ix had never experienced this even once in his life, but he nodded anyway.

"Indeed. Now, this concerns different countries, but there are some regions where the given name actually comes after the surname. Oh, how I have some amusing tales on that subject…"

At some point, Ix decided to cut off the small talk and get out of there.

Thinking it would be best to try the tea he'd been offered, he took a sip from his untouched beverage. The teacup was so fragile, it seemed liable to break were he to accidentally hit it on his teeth. He carefully set it back on the table.

"Right, so since I've delivered the letter…," announced Ix as he started to get up.

"Ah, well… You've come all this way, so why don't you take some time?" asked Elion, gently raising a hand to stop him. "In fact, would you like to attend today's banquet?"

"Sorry, but I've got other things to do today."

"Such as…meeting with Lady Saneeld?"

Ix stopped, then slowly sat down again. He leaned forward with his elbows on his knees, his hands folded, and asked, "…Was that written in the letter?"

"No, it wasn't. My apologies again, but as a merchant, you can't help but gather information, even when you're not trying to. She's faring quite poorly at the moment. I believe it would be near impossible for someone like you, an unrelated commoner, to form a connection with the Saneeld family. I imagine your friends at the library will be met with an unfavorable response."

"Thanks for the advice. Not that it's very useful…"

"However, the Obryle clan *can* form a connection with the Saneelds." Elion winked at Ix. "As a matter of fact, we already have, you see."

"What are you getting at?"

"Lady Saneeld herself will be attending the banquet tonight."

"…What about her health?"

"Yes, it is not ideal, but she has been doing relatively well the past few days. Her family has contacted us to confirm that she'll be attending. Assuming she doesn't take a sudden turn for the worse, that is."

"Isn't it just rich people who go? Nobles and merchants and those sorts… Wouldn't someone so obviously impoverished stick out like a sore thumb?"

"You don't necessarily have to attend the banquet. You could wait in this room—I will keep an eye out for an ideal moment and call you when it comes. An ill lady would want to rest at some point, so it would go unnoticed. I wouldn't mind if a friend tagged along, either. When it comes to social gatherings, the more the merrier."

"You probably don't know—"

"I am aware of your friend's birthplace."

"Well, that makes it easier…," said Ix, his eyebrows knit.

"Do you have any other concerns?"

"What do you want from me in return?"

"In return, oh my," said Elion with a chuckle and a wave of his hand. "This is for the capital's wand wall, the nation's security. Any citizen loyal to the king would provide such trifling assistance."

"You know about that, too…" Ix sighed. "If this was really for security purposes, someone who's actually in civil service would be carrying out the investigation, not me. Most of what I'm doing is just satisfying Layumatah's curiosity. You're probably aware of that already, too. That was a pretty warm welcome you gave me just for bringing you a letter. And I don't see what you could gain from helping out a measly apprentice like me. So there's got to be some sort of condition."

"Hmm, you are a suspicious one."

"I've had some pretty bad experiences. I'm just protecting myself by trying to avoid doing something foolish."

"I understand."

Elion gave a sad smile and stood. He asked Ix to wait a moment and left the room.

He wouldn't be back for a while. Ix finished drinking his tea, and just as he thought he might as well see himself out, the door opened again at last.

The face that appeared in the entryway belonged to a young boy of around ten years old. He had the same pale blond hair as Elion, and he was beaming from ear to ear. He looked directly at Ix.

"Ix," he said in a clear voice.

"Ottou?" muttered Ix.

This was the boy who went to Morna's shop to handle whatever she wasn't very good at, which was everything except crafting wands.

Elion also entered and stood behind Ottou, his hands on the boy's shoulders.

"This is the Obryle family's seventh son," announced Elion.

"…He's Ottou Obryle?"

"He is indeed."

"Uh-huh…"

"Our family treats him as though he doesn't exist. The only people who have shown him kindness are you and the people at the shop." Elion bowed his head low. "I am overwhelmed with gratitude toward you, Mr. Ix, and Ms. Morna as well, for always looking out for him. I thank you from the bottom of my heart."

"Well…"

Ix debated whether to tell Elion he was mixing things up, and that in truth, Ottou was looking after Morna. Ultimately, he gave a vague response in the form of holding up an open hand.

2

"Ottou's the Obryles'…?" asked Yuui with wide eyes.

"Son, apparently," confirmed Ix with a shrug. "Guess he's been coming here from that mansion every day. Morna, did you know about this?"

"Eh, huh, ah, um?"

Morna's eyes darted back and forth as they stared at her, but she was hemmed in on either side by them, so her pupils ended up bouncing between the floor and ceiling.

"I didn't tell her," added Ottou shortly.

"I do think there is a problem that she let him help without his family even knowing where he was…," said Yuui.

"Uh, uuuurgh…"

Everyone—Ix, Yuui, Nova, and now Ottou—had gathered again at Morna's store. Morna had been delighted to see Ottou for the first time in days, but after that, the conversation immediately swerved in this direction.

"You too, Ix. You've known Ottou for a while, haven't you?" asked Yuui as she pressed a hand to her forehead.

"It's not like I asked him for details on his family history," said Ix, no expression on his face. "I just thought he was a kid from a small merchant family."

"You never asked his surname?" asked Yuui.

"I don't care about that. Plus, there was a chance he wouldn't have one," said Ix.

"*Sigh…*"

©Enji

Yuui exhaled deeply. She hadn't asked Ottou, either, of course, but she would have thought Morna would have been informed at least.

How could it be this bad...?

Ottou was staring at Nova.

"What?" she asked with a tilt of her head.

Instead of answering, the boy shifted his gaze straight ahead.

Had the Obryle family really approved of their son coming to this shop? Regardless of the high quality of its product, from the outside, Morna's store looked like a poor, run-down excuse for a business. When Yuui inquired about this in a roundabout way, Ix said there was a reason for it.

Between what Elion said and what Ottou muttered at key points, Ix had concluded that Ottou was being raised as though he were illegitimate. His observational skills and memory may have far outstripped the norm, but he overdid it, so he couldn't carry a normal conversation. This meant the family didn't want to regard him as their own son. Few people outside the clan knew he existed, which was why Ottou hadn't revealed who he was, either.

Elion, the fourth son, was virtually the only one to interact with the boy at all, and he'd hid from the others the fact that Ottou was leaving the mansion. They normally kept him in a room deep within their estate, and no one went out of their way to go visit him.

"However," Elion had said, "to be honest, I don't believe Father is clueless about what's going on. I think it's likely he is aware but chooses to overlook it. Even if something happened to Ottou, say, a kidnapping, it wouldn't pose a threat to the family."

Elion was convinced that the Obryles even frowned on Ottou's talents and that he wouldn't be allowed to play a role in their business. That was why Elion was so grateful to Morna for accepting his brother. Normally, Elion had servants keep an eye on Ottou while he traveled to and from the shop, but they'd been so busy with preparations for the banquet the past few days that they couldn't spare the manpower, so Ottou needed to stay put in the mansion.

Yuui shook her head and gathered her thoughts.

"The new head librarian was useless, as we expected. He was able to deliver our message, true, but the answer he got was that outsiders would be unable to meet her. It will be a real boon if we can meet Lady Mali at this banquet. I am amazed Elion has helped this much, even if it is because of Ottou…"

"Though it seems he was interested in the witch as well," noted Ix.

"Why is that?"

"Because of the two adventurers you captured." He turned his eyes up. "The pair had a mountain of enedo teeth on them, right? Putting that much of a valuable product onto the market in one go would create chaos. And if the witch was aiming to destabilize the market, that could cause problems for merchants down the line."

"He even knew about that…?"

Morna's merchant contact was supposed to be slowly introducing that pile of enedo teeth into circulation. Perhaps you could expect a merchant from the clan who controlled the city to do as much.

"But about this banquet…," murmured Yuui. "It would be best if I don't attend."

"You won't leave the room," said Ottou.

"I know that, but there will be lots of people there. We can't be certain no one will see my face." What would happen if people realized there was an easterner in a place where some of the kingdom's most influential people were gathered? Yuui didn't have any trouble imagining it, but she couldn't tell just how big a problem it would become. "If it's merely to ask Lady Mali some questions, wouldn't Ix be plenty by himself? Ah, actually, you are a terrible conversationalist… Perhaps Nova should go along with you."

"I need her to come along with me either way," said Ix, which took Yuui off guard.

"What is this about? Are you that anxious?" she asked.

"Anxious?" asked Ix like he didn't understand. "Seems people normally go to these party things as a couple. Obviously, we'll be in a different room to talk to Mali, but we'll have to head down there to start talking to her. I'd stand out too much if I was on my own. Elion said he couldn't help me with that part."

"Ah, um..." Yuui searched for a response for a moment. "Clothes... Yes, what will you do about clothing? I'm sure you don't have any high-end outfits."

"Elion's going to lend me something. He can also give us women's wear."

"Oh, well then..."

"And we don't really have any other options for this," noted Ix flatly. "You can't do it, Yuui, for the exact reason you just said yourself."

"Yes..." She would have to show her face and skin dressed like that.

"And Morna—"

"M-m-me?!" she gasped, furiously waving her hands.

"Is an obvious no-go. So then—"

"I'll dress as a girl," announced Ottou out of the blue.

"Huh? That—" started Yuui.

"Too large a difference in height and age. It'd be unnatural," countered Ix, quickly shooting down that idea.

"I don't know if it would be that much of a problem...," said Yuui.

She tried imagining Morna with makeup and Ottou dressed as a girl. Ottou in feminine attire wouldn't be a problem. She thought he would make an enchanting little girl. And Morna, with her hair done, makeup, and nice clothing... She wouldn't look bad, either. Though her problems were on the inside, not the outside. If you threw her in a room with a bunch of strangers, she'd wind up doing more than just losing her lunch. What came after vomiting, you ask? Perhaps she would just explode. Anyway, pointless thought experiments aside...

©Enji

Yuui patted her cheeks and nodded.

"You're right—Nova is the only option," she said.

"And since she's a noble, she probably knows all the manners you need for these situations. So I want to ask you for your help. Do you have any issues with that?" Ix asked Nova.

"No."

"Uh, a-are you certain?" Yuui asked her again before she could stop herself.

"Yes. It is, part of the job."

"Oh, right…"

"Yuui, please come, too," requested Nova.

"Huh?"

"It would be faster, if we both ask questions."

"…All right."

When Yuui acquiesced, Ix raised an eyebrow in surprise.

"Sure that's okay?" he inquired.

"What?" she replied.

"Uh, nothing really."

"Nothing really what?"

3

That afternoon, a light rain began to fall. Several long sheets were passed over the courtyard and fastened to the railing on the second floor. Another rope was hung from above to pull them up in the middle. This would prevent water from pooling in the center by allowing it to run off the edge of the tarp.

"…We can't see what's happening in the courtyard like this," noticed Yuui. "Do you remember Lady Mali's face?"

"Pretty much," replied Ix with a nod. "Even if I can't figure out who she is, I can just look for an old woman who seems like she's about to keel over. Can't be too many of those."

"……"

Yuui fell silent, looking as though she was at a loss.

To her other side stood Nova, absentmindedly gazing down at the courtyard as well, or rather the sheets draped over it. She was still wearing her usual baggy attire. Ottou was also wearing his normal getup. He wouldn't be making an appearance at the banquet.

The four of them came to the Obryle mansion well before any of the other guests arrived. They entered through a back door that Ottou normally used to come and go, passing by bustling servants as they did. The servants had been told they were Elion's private guests.

Finally, the other attendees started to filter in. Voices, laughter, and other sounds that come with gatherings of people rang out on the second floor. The pattering of rain on the tarps above probably added to the atmosphere below.

A performance of musical instruments began. First there was just one melody; then a second joined in, until eventually there were layers of serene music floating up into the air. Every once in a while, there came a spatter of clapping hands.

Sometime after the banquet started, the voice of a man boomed. It seemed to be some sort of greeting. Applause showered his speech at multiple intervals. Up on the second floor, they could only hear bits and pieces, like "this year's festival" or "thanks for all your assistance."

If they were going to bring Mali upstairs, they would have to wait for a time when the banquet had been going for quite a while and it wouldn't cause a stir if she left early. They would likely be idling a while longer.

Ix went back to the room he was given for a bit so he could change clothes. He didn't even know how to put them on, but he managed to get into them with Ottou's help. Elion's clothes were a tad small for Ix, but they would have been tight even without that. The outfit constricted various parts of his body, so he found it hard to breathe. It featured lots of pointless frills and ornamentation and very few things you would normally need. Ix couldn't fathom why people liked wearing this type of thing. Maybe when you were rich, you started to see torture as beauty or your sensibilities flipped. Considering what he'd seen so far, Ix believed the latter was more likely.

Nova was also changing with Yuui's help. Women's clothing was even more complicated than menswear. Ix didn't think he would be able to get himself into some of that, even with Ottou's help.

When Yuui returned, she looked at Ix, and her jaw dopped.

"How should I put this...?" she said, looking uncertain. "I'm not sure I can say it suits you, but, well, it doesn't look unnatural, either."

"Yeah? It'll work, then. Nova, you all right, too?" asked Ix.

"Yes."

The outfit that had been prepared for Nova was slightly too large for her. Her hands were half hidden by the sleeves, and her eyes were obscured by her bangs as usual. It didn't seem to clash with her, though, perhaps because she was used to wearing finery.

The rain steadily grew in intensity, though it still wasn't very strong. The banquet was continuing without issue.

"About time," murmured Ottou when he looked downstairs.

"How's it look?" asked Ix.

"Overall movement has decreased. Many attendees are chatting in groups or resting. A few of them will leave soon," the boy answered in an even tone.

"Mali?"

"Probability is low."

"Thanks, Ottou," said Ix. Then he turned to Nova and said, "Let's go."

"Yes."

They went downstairs and walked along the path that circled the courtyard. There were several lights set up throughout the courtyard, but they threw that path into shadow, allowing Ix and Nova to avoid notice. Servants passed them on hurried feet.

They observed the party. Each and every person wore a resplendent outfit and was engaged in friendly chatter. As Ix had been told before, most of the attendees were moving around in pairs of one man and one woman. Because this was a pre-party for the harvest festival, there were mounds of succulent meat in one section of the courtyard. There were other steaming dishes as well, but it seemed like they had barely been touched. Evidently, conversation took priority for these people.

After examining the attendees' tight-fitting clothing, Ix suddenly cocked his head in confusion.

"…Where do you put a wand in that kind of clothing?" he asked.

"You, don't," replied Nova immediately.

"Hmm? Why not?"

"It is, incredibly rude to bring a weapon, to a social event. Most people would, come without a wand, or, leave it with the host when they arrive. Only the guards, can have one."

"And where are they?"

"They should be, on the perimeter. They do not, come into the banquet."

"Is there any point in having security, then?"

At that point, Nova looked at him wordlessly. Then she said, "…Ix, you have no mana, right?"

"Hmm? Yeah, that's right…"

During their conversation, Ix and Nova had turned two corners around the square, putting them almost directly across from where they'd looked down from the balcony before.

They walked down about a third of that side when Ix stopped.

"I think that's her," he said quietly as he pointed. "Sitting there."

Nova nodded but didn't speak.

An elderly woman in purple sat in a chair on the periphery. She was short and had long white hair. Beside her stood a stout lady who spoke to the older one occasionally. She was probably an attendant, not a guest.

Ix and Nova watched until the other people in the area dispersed somewhat, then stepped into the courtyard. They walked over casually.

The elderly woman noticed them first. Ix didn't remember her face very well, but he knew those eyes. Golden eyes that shone like a child's.

The attendant noticed the woman looking in their direction. She smiled gently and stepped between her and them as Ix and Nova approached.

"Good evening. May I ask who—?"

"Are you Mali Saneeld?" inquired Ix in a low voice, ignoring the attendant.

The attendant's brow furrowed in annoyance. She loudly cleared her throat and said, "Excuse me—"

"Yes, I am," replied Mali as she gently raised a hand. The attendant looked up to the sky in exasperation and stepped aside.

"You the noble who did some work on the wand wall sixty years ago?" asked Ix.

"I am."

"We want to ask you about it."

"Bryan gave me your message," said Mali as she stood with the attendant's help. "Shall we move elsewhere to talk? I presume you have a room prepared?"

"I want to confirm one thing first," said Ix.

"What is that?"

Ix stared directly at her, then said, "Are you the witch?"

Her large eyes twinkled.

Her expression was unreadable; then, slowly, she spoke.

"No, I am not."

"But that means you've heard of the witch?"

"You only said there was one thing you wanted to check."

4

The attendant tried to follow Mali, but the elderly woman left her on the first floor and came up to the room alone. The guests around her didn't question it when she said she was going to take a rest. They seemed to assume that Ix and Nova were some kind, plain young folks helping her. She was legitimately unsteady on her feet, though, so Ix lent her a hand as they climbed the stairs.

Mali sat in a chair next to the window and fixed her eyes on them. Ix and Yuui sat across from her. Nova was in a corner, and Ottou stood by the window, staring out.

Now that they could get a good look at her, Mali appeared to have aged significantly since they last saw her only a few months ago. Her movements were weak, and her body seemed shrunken into itself. Sometimes, she would place a hand on her chest and let out a painful-sounding cough.

"I apologize for bringing you here all of a sudden," said Yuui with a bow of her head. "I understand it is rude of us, but we would be grateful if you would answer some questions."

"I don't particularly mind," replied Mali. She took a slow sip from the water they gave her, then let out a heavy sigh. "Who are you, by the way?"

"I'm an apprentice wandmaker. Layumatah, who studied under the same craftsman as me, asked me to look into something with you," replied Ix.

"The girl over there and I are lending a hand," added Yuui.

"Layumatah… She is one of Munzil's apprentices, I believe. The message I received said you wanted to ask about the wand wall," said Mali.

Ix cut immediately to the chase and said, "There's a chance the wand wall in the capital has been undone."

"Hmph. Not good, if it's true." Mali nodded, her expression unchanged.

"That's why Layumatah did a bit of digging of her own. She discovered that the emission method was used on the wand wall during some repairs sixty years ago. But the thing is, that was thirty years before the emission method went into widespread use. With a bit more detailed investigation, she found there was a young noble involved with the project, someone who wasn't a wandmaker. Mali Saneeld was her name."

"I see. Well investigated. Does that mean you suspect me?"

"To be honest, I've ruled you out when it comes to the wall. You've been in Leirest for the past few years as the head librarian. And though you retired recently because of your poor health, you wouldn't have time to get all the way to the capital. I doubt you have anything to do with it. That should be enough to convince Layumatah."

"I would appreciate it if you could lay that out to her. As you can probably tell, I don't have the strength to travel long distances to explain myself or be interrogated. And if you deem me a suspect, I would likely die during the investigation."

"Which is why that's not what we want to ask about." Ix shook his head.

Mali took another drink of water.

It had grown dark outside. All they could hear was the sound of the rain. The bright candles in the room cast wavering shadows over Mali's face.

"Apparently, my master had told Layumatah that a witch designed the capital's wand wall." Ix fixed his eyes on her. "I'm not going to beat around the bush. Are you the *witch* who implemented the emission method?"

"I am not. I said as much earlier."

"But you know about the witch?"

"I do."

"Have you met her?"

"Yes."

"In Notswoll?"

"......"

That was the first time Mali's expression visibly changed. Her eyes widened, and she fixed a sharp glare at them.

"You don't need to hide it. Or rather, we'd already gathered that much," continued Ix. "The witch is a powerful magic user who lives in the forest by Notswoll. When did you meet her? Can't imagine what reason a noble from Leirest would have for going to a backwater village."

"I imagine you'd want an answer for that," said Mali.

"Ottou," called Ix, and the boy immediately turned to face him. Ix gestured toward Mali and asked, "What about her?"

Ottou immediately said, "From the time she was a child until the time she was near adulthood, she lived in a village near Leirest. She came to the city proper afterward and has remained here ever since."

"...What is this?" asked Mali with a shake of her head. "Even the Obryle family shouldn't be able to have gleaned that from their investigations."

"It wasn't from an investigation. Ottou just analyzed your speech and mannerisms to draw a conclusion. He can do that kind of thing," explained Ix casually. "So until she was an adult... That lines up with my calculation."

Yuui cocked her head, wondering what he meant.

"The Notswoll witch eats people, right?" he explained. "Her most recent victim was a baby twenty years ago. Before that, a girl was devoured about eighty years back. And the work on the wand wall happened sixty years ago. That comes out to just about two decades. But say the girl who the witch should have gobbled up returned after twenty years to work on the wall with some special knowledge she'd obtained... From there it's easy to connect the dots."

Ix looked at Mali as if to ask what she thought, and she clamped her mouth shut.

In reality, Ix wasn't certain of his conjecture. Most of it was inferences that had just occurred to him on the spot, including the calculation. If someone came back and demanded proof of what he said, he'd have to give up then and there.

But Mali hung her head somewhat. She let out a heavy sigh. She shrank deeper into herself, and for a brief moment, Ix worried that she might just compress into nothingness.

"You really have done your research," she said in a voice that had to be squeezed out of her body.

"So you admit it?" asked Ix.

"Yes, it is as you say."

"What part?"

"…May I have some more water?"

"Ah, y-yes," said Yuui.

She quickly picked up Mali's empty glass and rushed off to the water jug set out earlier. Seeing her do that, Ix realized that he was hungry. Now that he thought about it, they had been waiting on the second floor this whole time and hadn't eaten dinner. Yuui and Ottou had to be starving, too. It would be a good idea to grab some food the next time he went downstairs. There was so much left from the banquet, he couldn't imagine anyone would have any objections.

Mali accepted the water from Yuui with a "thank you" and took several sips.

"…To be honest, I've wanted to reveal this to someone for ages," she said.

"You're going to tell us?" asked Ix.

"I was born into the Saneeld family here in Leirest," she started quietly. "Before I was even old enough to have memories of the city, I was sent to Notswoll. To the public, I was just a commoner's child, and that was how I would be raised. At the time, I didn't understand why things had to be that way, but to keep things simple, it was so that I could escape a power struggle within the family. Not long after I was born, there were multiple attempts on my life, so my mother decided to send me away. A servant was sent away with me to act as my guardian. Naturally, the villagers realized there was something unusual about my circumstances. The children sensed it as well, and I was often excluded from their friend groups. Thinking back to it now, it was such a minor thing, but I suffered quite a bit as a girl. Of course, financially speaking, I was free of hardship."

Mali still gripped the empty glass with both hands.

"That was when I met her. Ah, yes, the witch. It was this time of year. Notswoll was in the middle of celebrating the Feast of Meat. That was the first year I attended the festival. And why was that? For some reason, I thought I could enjoy the celebration as well that year. Just as it was drawing to a close, the witch appeared. I still remember it... There was a great storm, and it brought her with it. The villagers and children were terrified and fled. But, as I explained, I was alienated from the rest of Notswoll. I'd never heard about the witch before. I didn't understand what everyone was afraid of. I didn't know. I didn't know the witch ate people. I thought it strange that everyone seemed frightened... I tried speaking with her, and I asked her to take me with her. The witch was kind, and she explained that she would consume me. At the time, I was okay with that."

She turned her distant gaze out the window. Nevertheless, her voice was smooth and confident as she told the story, belying her age and condition.

"But you're still alive," said Ix.

"Yes...I am. The witch took me to her home, but she didn't devour me immediately. She didn't explain why. She just said it would be '*a waste to eat you now*.' I lived in that house in the forest with her like that for nearly the next two decades. A few years after I passed into adulthood, I left the forest. Or rather, I was chased out."

"Chased out?" asked Yuui.

"I'm embarrassed to admit it, but I grew frightened. She told me that she would soon eat me. Yes, after spending twenty years there, I could endure it no longer. I was terrified. I didn't want that to happen; I couldn't help myself. So I waited for the right moment and snuck away from the woods. But there was a family I didn't know living in my house in the village, and the servant who had come with me originally had apparently passed. What would you expect? Everyone thought I was dead, that I had been gobbled up." Mali smiled bitterly.

"With no other choice, I relied on my faint memories from when I was a young child and made my way to Leirest. Ah, how I remember that journey. Walking along muddy paths, not knowing if I'd chosen the correct street. But somehow, I made it. I visited the Saneeld mansion and told them I was a daughter of their clan. No one believed me at first, but I was able to prove it with the sole family crest I'd been made to keep with me. By then, the feud in house Saneeld had long since ended. My mother emerged victorious and selected another successor in my place, having thought me dead. I needed to prove my worth in order to earn a place in the family. That's when I heard about the construction on the wand wall."

"Then the emission method—"

"Came from the witch's knowledge, as you already learned. I had many opportunities to see her magic over the twenty years I spent with her. I didn't understand most of it, but I could do a few of her tricks. The emission method was one of the things I'd learned. It was my only lifeline. I told the others it was strictly confidential and implemented the technique on the wand wall during the repairs. The craftsmen didn't seem to understand it, either, but they were convinced when I demonstrated the potential results for them. That is the entirety of my experience."

The room was silent for a while.

Mali had no reason to lie, and no one could improvise such a long, cohesive yarn. Setting aside the possibility of misremembered details, what she had just told was the truth.

Which meant it was proof.

The witch ate people. The rumor was true.

And her knowledge was thirty years ahead of humanity's, at the very least.

At this point, you couldn't just dismiss the tales as impossible or absurd.

"The witch…is in Notswoll, yeah?" asked Ix, though the answer was obvious.

"Yes, she is. I'm sure she still is," responded Mali. Her tone was so natural that at first he didn't notice the tears spilling from her eyes. "Which is why I am not the witch. I…I just ran. She spent twenty years with me and…I betrayed her. In the end I was just…weak and scared…"

"Y-you didn't betray her," said Yuui. "She would have devoured you. Anyone would have been frightened. There's no need to feel embarrassed about running. It is an entirely normal reaction. You shouldn't blame yourself…"

"But…I told her. The day we met, I told her. That I didn't mind… I did, I know I did…"

5

They waited for Mali to regain her composure before Ix took her back downstairs. He was just tagging along to help her down the stairs, so Nova said it would be fine if she didn't accompany them.

He held her wrinkled hand as they descended step by step. It felt much stronger than he'd imagined it would be based on appearance alone.

Mali's attendant was waiting at the bottom of the staircase. Ix remembered he'd thought about getting some food for everyone.

"What's the matter?" asked Mali as she looked at him.

"It's just…I want to take some food from the banquet upstairs, but it'll look suspicious if I do, since I'll have to take enough for four people," replied Ix.

"You could ask the servants to take some up."

"Oh yeah...," he said, realizing that this was how rich people thought.

"You can ask her for help," said Mali, pointing to the attendant who was looking up at them with relief on her face.

"You sure?"

"Thanks to all of you, I was able to remember my mistakes. This is nothing."

They never did get their dinner in the end.

With Mali's help, Ix asked the servants to bring up the grub. It was decided they would get food directly from the kitchen rather than what was laid out in the courtyard. He waited on the path for a while so he could escort them to the room, but they didn't show. Then he started to worry they might actually be cooking fresh food.

That's when an argument broke out at one of the doors leading into the mansion.

Ix moved closer and saw a servant standing in front of the entrance, wearing an anxious expression with his arms spread wide. In front of him was a group of people voicing complaints. Apparently, they couldn't get out.

Ix decided he was unlikely to draw attention to himself with this going on, so he quickly spoke to a nearby guest.

"What's going on?" he asked.

"I'm not sure—I only just came over myself...," replied the attendee. He shot a quick glance at Ix but then turned his eyes back immediately. "There was something about poison, and we've been asked not to leave."

"Poison?"

A moment later, other servants came through the door into the courtyard. A few of them looked alarmed as they shooed away the bystanders. Most of the attendees seemed to have no idea what was going on and walked away in confusion.

"My apologies, everyone. I am one of the kitchen staff," said the servant at the door, this time raising his voice. "A mistake occurred during cooking, which has resulted in a poisonous gas in the kitchen. It is usually harmless, but breathing in large quantities may have health impacts. We are currently ventilating the gas, and I appreciate your patience as we do."

There were a few grumbles, but most of the guests seemed satisfied with the explanation. They returned to the courtyard with unconcerned expressions, looking at the ones still hanging on and frowning in disapproval. The people still complaining noticed those grimaces and backed off as well. One man, who might have been a member of the Obryle family, quickly approached the servant.

With that, Ix decided he couldn't expect a meal anytime soon. He decided to go back to the room for now and tried to go up the stairs, but another servant barred the way. This one was a woman.

"I want to go upstairs," said Ix.

He could feel suspicious eyes gathering on him from the other attendees, who might have suspected he would cause a scene.

"My apologies, sir, please wait here," she replied.

"Why? If it's safe here, the second floor should be all right, too."

"I have simply been given orders to that effect. I am sorry, but please wait in the courtyard."

"Right…"

There wasn't much he could do if she insisted. He was about to go back to a corner and stand there but struck up a casual conversation with the servant instead.

"You all take care of many sorts of jobs, don't you?" he asked.

"Sir?" The woman blinked in confusion. "Oh, yes… We do. Currently I'm acting as a waiter, but normally I'm a cleaner."

"What about gardening?"

"Hmm?"

"You were in the garden this morning, weren't you? You were wearing coveralls. Were you cleaning it? I assume that's usually a specialized job…"

The woman looked at him with her head cocked for a few seconds, then drew something long and thin from her inside pocket.

Ix wondered what it could possibly be but quickly realized it was an object he was very familiar with.

It was a smooth, worked stick—a wand.

Just as he was wondering if it was okay for the servants to carry wands while the guests couldn't, the tip of the instrument glowed. He closed his eyes against the blinding light.

When he opened them, he was lying on the ground on his stomach, his cheek pressed against the courtyard's stone pavement.

Maybe he'd collapsed in surprise from the brightness? He must have hit his head as well; his vision was hazy, and his body felt numb and wouldn't move properly.

Ix managed to plant his hands on the ground and slowly push himself up. After shaking his head many times, he squeezed his eyes shut. Now things were finally clear.

...*What the hell am I doing?*

Surely everyone should have been staring at him, since he'd fallen over, but for some reason, not a single person in view was looking his way. In fact, everyone was sitting on the ground in neat rows. It was an unusual sight. They were dirtying the fancy clothes they'd all made a point of wearing. Though, if their sensibilities were backward, then maybe they thought it was okay to soil expensive clothing. Perhaps this, too, was something you did at banquets for the rich.

Just then, something struck him in the back, and he fell forward.

Turning around, Ix saw another servant standing there, gazing down at him. He had a wand in his right hand. He told Ix to stand.

Ix stood, realizing the man had pushed him. The fancy clothing Ix had borrowed had gotten dirty. He tried to wipe it off, but it was no use. That wasn't good.

"Walk," ordered the man as he pressed the wand to Ix's back.

"What's go—?"

"Walk."

The man pushed on Ix's back, and he stumbled. He had a coughing fit. A few of the people sitting in rows glanced at him.

It seemed the man was ordering Ix to join the collection of

people. He did as instructed and walked to the end of one of the rows, then sat down. There were three rows in total, and everyone was facing sideways. Mali and her attendant were also there, diagonally in front of him. It wasn't just the guests in the row, either—there were servants lined up as well. A quick look around told Ix that they were surrounded by several other servants.

"A-are you all right?" came a quiet whisper.

Ix turned around and saw the guest who'd told him about the poison. He seemed tense.

"All right?" asked Ix in confusion.

"Well, you… A spell hit you and knocked you back. You laid there convulsing for such a long time that I started to think you wouldn't make it…"

"……"

"Ah, don't force yourself to speak if you're still unwell." The man opened his hand. "But good job…or maybe that's not the right thing to say. Well spotted, actually. Oh right, my name is Marlan. Uh, are you a member of the Obryle family?"

"…I'm Ix."

"Mr. Ix, you must have eagle eyes, ha-ha…ha."

The crowd suddenly started buzzing. One of the servants surrounding the courtyard stepped forward and glared down at them. He was fairly old with a bald head.

"Everyone, I apologize for scaring you, but we are enacting God's will. I believe that those of you who, like us, have taken their purification will approve of our beliefs soon enough," he said as he spread his arms.

6

After Ix and Mali left the room, only the three of them remained. Yuui stayed put in the same chair as before, while Ottou and Nova kept standing in their respective locations. Yuui started to feel uncomfortable and decided it might be better to get up.

"Well, we've accomplished what we came here for," she remarked, glancing at Nova. "The investigations into the mystery of the wand wall and Mali have concluded. That should be plenty to report back to Layumatah with."

"Yes."

"What will you do next, Nova?"

"What, do you mean?"

"Ix will likely head to Notswoll. My original target was the witch as well, so I plan to join him. But your work here is done. I was wondering if we would part ways here and you would return to the capital."

"I will, go, too," said Nova immediately.

"Oh, well then, I look forward to working with you a little longer."

"Yes," she replied, then she paused in confusion. "You're certain, Ix will go to Notswoll?"

"Yes, he has his own reasons."

"I see."

"Gidens was heading back to the village tomorrow morning, correct? Shall we ask if we can accompany him?"

Nova nodded slightly, and the conversation ended.

The room returned to silence. Quite some time passed, but Ix didn't return. For all they knew, he could have gotten dragged into something dangerous while he was taking Mali back. It was a brief window of time for something like that to happen, but with him, anything was possible.

"Nova, I hate to ask, but," said Yuui, "could you go downstairs and look for Ix?"

"Yes."

Just as she was about to leave the room, they heard a huge explosion.

It sounded like it had come from downstairs. Then the noise cut off, and they heard nothing further.

"What was that?" asked Yuui.

The walls and door of this chamber were quite thick, preventing sound from passing through. With the entrance closed as it was, they couldn't make out anything going on downstairs. That meant the explosion they'd heard must have been incredibly loud.

Nova took her hand away from the doorknob and pressed her ear to the door.

"Magic," said Ottou suddenly.

"Huh?" Yuui looked back at the window. "But no one is allowed to bring a wand onto the premises."

"Prohibited and difficult to manage." Ottou spoke at a steady pace. "The guests are searched using magic. Someone may have been able to get one or two wands inside. With that many, they would be arrested the moment security noticed."

"Hmm, perhaps there was some sort of accident..."

"Someone's coming," stated Nova as she moved away from the door.

"Is it Ix?" asked Yuui.

"I don't, know."

"Of course."

Yuui got up and moved to the middle of the room so that she was vaguely standing in front of Ottou. She gently gripped the wand hidden inside her pocket. Nova stood near the door, her posture the same as always.

Shortly after, the door opened slowly from the other side.

"Ah, guests...?" said the man as he peeked in. He looked like a servant. He came into the room, and the door naturally swung closed. "My apologies, but could everyone come down to the courtyard?"

"Why?" asked Yuui. "We weren't formally invited here. We wouldn't want to impose on the other attendees."

"There's been a small incident. The second floor may not be safe."

"An incident? What happened?"

"There was a mistake made by the cooking staff... That is why we're requesting everyone to move to safety, starting from the kitchen first."

"The kitchen?" Yuui tilted her head.

"Yes."

"But then, what was that magic used in the courtyard a moment ago?"

"Ah, there was a scuffle among some of the guests, but there's no need to worry about that. It's been taken care of."

"Is that so," wondered Yuui as she steadied her breathing. "Ottou, what about this man?"

"Incorrect," came the boy's voice.

Yuui felt the flow of mana and immediately drew her wand to cast a spell.

A blinding light filled the room, and a burning smell wafted up to her a moment afterward.

Yuui and the man stood, each leveling a wand at the other. The floor between them was blackened and burned, though the damage was much closer to the assailant.

He gave Yuui a sharp glare, as though questioning why she would have been armed. He squeezed tightly onto his wand.

Opposing him, Yuui was so calm, it surprised even her. This was the first time she'd used magic in a real fight, but she felt no panic. That last clash of spells had made their difference in power clear. He was far too weak.

Actually, it was his wand that was lacking. Or more accurately, Yuui's wand was far too powerful. Claiming all that as her own strength would be arrogant. This was borrowed power, magic from a dragon.

This was the wand that held a dragon's heart.

The instrument was overwhelmingly superior to his in both how long it took to cast a spell and in its mana transmission efficiency. Yuui had so much leeway that she'd been able to adjust the power of her spell so that it would only cancel her opponent's

incantation, rather than kill him outright. She hadn't wanted to take him out with the first shot because she still wasn't absolutely certain he was her enemy.

Even so, she couldn't let her guard down. There were no certainties in battle. That was true of a one-on-one fight, but she also had Nova and Ottou here. If a spell went awry, it could put them in harm's way. The first thing Yuui needed to do was to get Nova to move to another location, since her friend was even closer to the man than she was.

Spells were cast at a straight line out of the tip of the user's wand, so both Yuui and her opponent had their eyes glued to the other's weapon.

"I'm sorry," Nova suddenly whispered.

"Huh, wha—?" The man stared in astonishment.

Where could Nova possibly have been hiding the short wand she now held? Naturally, the tip was pointed directly at the assailant's face.

Losing his composure, the man pulled back. Yuui sensed the flow of mana. She quickly aimed her wand at her opponent's hand, but—

The next moment, he flew backward.

"Huh?" gasped Yuui.

His back crashed into the wall, and he slid limply to the ground.

A wand clattered to the floor at almost the exact same instant.

Nova now stood in the spot where the man had been a moment before. Her knees were arched to lower her center of gravity, and her bent elbow was thrust forward.

It took a few seconds to realize what had happened. Nova had tossed her wand to draw the man's attention upward. With that opening, she'd slipped into a fighting stance and moved closer, then sent him flying backward with an elbow strike. The man was now sprawled across the floor, unconscious.

"Let's tie him, up," suggested Nova as she came out of her stance and turned toward Yuui.

They grabbed the cloth in the room to bind his hands and feet, plus gag him. Yuui picked up his wand and put it in her pocket.

She found herself staring at Nova, wondering where she'd been hiding such strength in her tiny frame. Beyond that, using your wand as a distraction was a tactic that didn't come naturally to magic users. There was no way Nova was just a student.

"I'm not sure this is the right time or place to ask this"—Yuui sighed—"but you were really sent to monitor me, weren't you?"

"Yes," confirmed Nova with a nod.

"You befriended me for that purpose?"

"Yes."

"And the stall incident was to draw me in?"

"That was just, my inexperience." Nova shook her head. "I was following you, and accidentally, got caught up. But since you saved me, I decided it would be easier, to get close to you."

"Is that so…? Well, that was some incredible unarmed defense."

"It is only because I have, taken special training. I myself, am not incredible."

"I'm not sure you have to say 'only' in this situation…"

"I apologize, for deceiving you." Nova lowered her head.

Yuui was surprised, but she found herself nodding. To be honest, she'd had an inkling of Nova's true nature from the day they met. There was no way Yuui would so conveniently find a new friend. She was a hostage, after all, and she'd done too much on her own over the summer. You could say she'd expected to be monitored eventually. She wasn't in a position to complain about it.

The Yuui from before would have been hurt by the fact that their entire friendship was a lie to facilitate Nova's surveillance, but the present Yuui didn't mind that much. That was probably thanks to the strength she'd found over the summer.

She stared at Nova's face. Oddly enough, Nova gazed back at her. Her expression and tone were both exactly the same as before.

"Anyway, right now we need to get a grip on what's happening," remarked Yuui with a shrug. From a different angle, it was actually very reassuring to have someone like Nova in this situation. "That man was probably on patrol. I imagine the courtyard has already been seized..."

"I, agree," said Nova, pressing her ear to the door again and blinking several times.

"But how did they defeat the guards at an event of this size? Shouldn't there be powerful magic users on watch?"

"There have been no sounds, of battle other than that spell, from before. I think, security doesn't know, what's happening yet."

"But you'd think they would notice soon enough—"

"They have hostages," interjected Ottou, jumping into the conversation.

"So they're seeking to negotiate? Hmm..."

Yuui placed a hand on her chin and thought. She didn't get anything about the situation. There was no reason to attack an event as highly guarded as this, out of all other options. And even if their negotiations succeeded, escape would prove difficult at best. She didn't know who was demanding what, but it would have been easier to pick off individuals as they moved about.

Suddenly, she realized the enemy was likely few in number. That would fit with Ottou's theory of them smuggling in a wand or two. They would be at an advantage if they were attacking an area where many people were gathered. But no, she still couldn't see the point in that. There were so many guards. Even if they took hostages, they wouldn't be able to handle all of security.

"I am having a hard time wrapping my head around this. What about the two of you?" asked Yuui.

Nova and Ottou stared silently at her. That probably meant they had no ideas. If these two couldn't hit on it, no one could.

"I will go, alert the guards. We should leave this, to them," said Nova as she took a step. "You two, wait here and hide."

"I agree we should leave this to security, but we can't hide.

They'll send another person on patrol when this one doesn't come back," said Yuui.

"It would be more dangerous for all three of us, to go. I'm sorry, but you two, can't come."

"What do you mean?"

"When you go down the stairs, you're on the path that surrounds, the courtyard. They would find you. I can't use that route. So, I will climb up, and go across the roof."

It impressed Yuui that Nova was capable of such an acrobatic feat. She hoped she could get Nova to show her when they had the opportunity. But now wasn't the time for that.

"We have other options," added Ottou. "If they send another patrol, we can still deal with just two people. We could draw their attention with the tied-up man and attack them from behind. That should give us enough time to last until the guards arrive."

"Yes, that is another, course of action," said Nova with a nod.

"We don't know when the interlopers downstairs will get desperate. I am opposed to a plan that just buys time," said Yuui.

The panic that she hadn't felt at all before was starting to catch up with her. There was a large number of hostages downstairs, many of whom were elderly, like Mali. They probably couldn't last being bound for long, assuming they hadn't been harmed in any other way.

And most importantly…was Ix.

There was no one in the world better at rubbing people the wrong way than him. Yuui could easily imagine him saying something stupid like "what a shit wand" to one of the attackers and pissing them off. But unlike the rest of the guests, he was neither noble nor merchant. He was a commoner, someone who had no value as a hostage. His captors might kill him to set an example if they discovered that.

Yuui raised her head and said, "Is there any way for us to save everyone?"

"Why?" asked Nova, glancing back at her.

"…What?" Yuui didn't understand the question Nova bounced

back at her. "Why? Because there are people in danger, and I want to try and save them…"

"All those people, are kingdom citizens."

"Well, it is a kingdom banquet."

"What I mean is, there is no gain for you, Yuui. In fact, you would be saving citizens from an enemy nation. That could be a loss for you, in the bigger picture."

"That's…" Yuui groped for words. "But it's the right thing to do, yes?"

"The right thing?" Nova asked back as if she didn't understand.

"Yes. My father left me that request, to be a good person."

"He requested that you, help the people on the side of your enemy, like you helped me?"

"…Why are you asking me this?" Yuui shook her head slightly. "Father… Yes, maybe saving kingdom citizens is not what he meant, but even so, I…"

Nova stared at Yuui for a while before she finally nodded.

"…Understood. Let's save, everyone."

Her bangs swayed, and Yuui saw her eyes for a brief moment.

7

What a shit wand, thought Ix.

He was referring to the wand the older man who'd stepped to the front was holding. It was so horribly worked that Ix was starting to doubt it was even real. The wand the woman had used to blast him backward earlier was far superior. Ix didn't have anything in particular to do right now, so he was spending his time staring at their equipment.

As Ix sat there bored, the older man launched into some speech after addressing the hostages, which Ix couldn't make hide or hair of. It wasn't like the man was using words he didn't understand;

he got the gist of his individual sentences just fine. But the man was splicing in so many indirect phrases and excessive flourishes to his statement that Ix couldn't put it all together.

If he had to sum up the spiel, it seemed like the man was insisting they cancel this year's Feast of Meat. He claimed they wouldn't become violent or kill the hostages if they refused their demands, just that no one could leave, and he would continue to persuade them until they were on the same page. The way Ix saw things, that in itself would probably constitute an act of violence, but no one pointed that out.

The speech dragged on for a long while before coming to an abrupt conclusion. Maybe it was just Ix who thought that, though. Whatever the case, the man briefly disappeared into the hall.

The guests whispered to one another. Ix caught snippets, such as "the Obryles' responsibility" or "the guards."

A commotion erupted behind him. He turned discreetly to catch a glimpse and saw a small figure standing on the stairs. It was Nova. Two servants hedged her in.

"I was resting in a room," Ix could hear her say.

"Didn't a man come to find you?" asked one of the servants.

"A, man? No, I didn't see, anyone."

"Really?"

"Yes."

"……"

The two servants looked at each other. After exchanging a few words, one pointed in Ix's direction and gestured with their chin. Nova gave a small nod and walked over, where she took a seat next to him.

"Are you, all right?" she asked in a quiet voice.

"Someone asked me the same thing earlier," he replied with a shrug. "Why'd you come down? Right now, there's—"

"I have a general grasp, of the situation. A man came patrolling earlier, on the second floor, but we took him out. Yuui and I have wands."

"How is she?"

"Uninjured."

"But they'll probably send someone else when their patrol doesn't come back."

"It should be all right, for a little while." Nova's tone was flat. "Normally, someone who defeated a patrol, wouldn't come down like this. They will likely, interpret it in a more convenient way."

"Like he's busy stealing valuables?"

"Yes."

"Is that why you came down? To buy Yuui and Ottou time?"

"No, we have another objective."

Ix looked around them. Many of the guests were talking to each other, their expressions serious, but the servants didn't seem to care. It would probably be all right.

"And that is?" he asked.

"The tarp will fall soon."

"Huh?"

Nova turned her eyes upward. She was talking about the long, thin sheets of cloth that had been hung across the second floor to act as a rain guard. There still seemed to be a slight drizzle, since they could hear the pattering of rain drops.

"Yuui will set it all loose, at once. Chaos will ensue."

"Probably, yeah."

"During the confusion, we will capture their leader. Both sides will have hostages, but the noise should alert the guards. If they come, we win."

"And who exactly is the 'we' in 'we will capture their leader'?"

"Me."

"...Can you do that?"

"Yes," replied Nova matter-of-factly. "Is their leader, that bald man up front?"

"Seems like it."

Ix decided that Nova coming down here meant that Yuui had agreed to the plan. If Nova said she could do it, she could.

"I can't believe a rich person's mansion got captured so easily," Ix said with a snort. "Aren't places like this supposed to have all sorts of security measures?"

"They probably didn't approach from the front," said Nova.

"Then how'd they do it?"

"...Before siege wands were developed, there were two ways of defeating a secured fortress." Nova's voice was emotionless. "Wait until the entrenched enemy's rations ran out or have someone on the inside to open the way. If the latter succeeded, the castle would soon fall."

"So they had a collaborator lying in wait who let them in? And that person did it all by themselves?"

"They would probably hire temporary help for the feast. And if the employer trusted one of the collaborators, that would be enough to bring in the others." Nova pulled her chin in slightly. "But I think in this instance, instead of having someone infiltrate, they..."

"A guess is fine—don't stop in the middle."

"Yes. They probably turned someone already working here, into a collaborator. That route is both simpler, and less wasteful."

"I would've thought that would be more difficult."

"It's the same as when you attack, a castle's walls. You look for a weak point, then strike there. It's a simple skill. Anyone can re-create it so long as they have training and a contact point," said Nova soberly. "For example, fortress under lockdown might still allow merchants in, so you could put a letter in with their goods. Throughout the history of war, there are instances where the soldiers who inspected those goods, or their superiors, betrayed their fellows."

"That kind of thing taught at the Academy?" asked Ix in a tone filled with both awe and exasperation.

"Yes."

"Hmph..."

He cast his eyes around the area. The tension seemed to have lifted slightly. The guests' conversations were becoming louder, so no one noticed their own, since it was mixed in with the chatter.

"It's a little surprising, though," said Nova.

"What is?" said Ix.

"That there are this few, people with wands." Nova tilted her head. "Ottou said there were maybe two or three wands. I didn't expect every person, to have one. Maybe we should cancel the plan."

"Wait..." Ix put a hand over his mouth. "Did he really say that?"

"Yes."

Ix blinked a few times.

Ottou was never off base about anything. If he said there were only two or three people with wands, then there were only two or three people with wands.

Which meant...

"Nova, how long do we have before your plan starts?" Ix asked quickly.

"Very, little time."

"Act like you're collapsing and knock me over."

"Yes," she responded immediately, without questioning him.

Unsteadily, she moved closer to Ix, who fell over on his back.

"What's going on?!" came a shout, and one of the servants came over.

"I don't have any strength," said Ix, coming up with some random explanation as he stared at the individual's hands. Placing a palm on his forehead, Ix got up slowly and checked each of the servants around him.

Right...

Apparently, they'd been holding his brain hostage as well.

He'd been on the inside the whole time, without any way out.

Being hit by a spell had left him muddled, but still, he couldn't believe he hadn't noticed this before.

"Here," said Nova as she held a hand out to him.

"Your target isn't the man from before," whispered Ix in her ear as he accepted her hand. "It's the woman hiding behind that pillar."

"Why?"

"She's the only one with a real wand."

"And, the others?"

"Plain old sticks."

"You're, certain?"

"It's obvious. As far as I can see anyway."

"Understood."

But something else unexpected happened before they could put their plan into motion.

Mali, who was sitting kitty-corner in front of them, suddenly pressed her hand to her chest and doubled over. She let out a faint groan amid ragged breaths. Her attendant knelt beside her and rubbed her back. Then she looked around, her expression dire. A servant approached them.

"She's unwell," stated Mali's attendant sharply. "She needs to take her medicine and get some rest."

"Nobody leaves until the Feast of Meat is canceled."

"How could you!" she cried bitterly. "How could you stand and watch someone die like this? Didn't you say you wouldn't do anything violent?"

"No one's harmed her."

"Refusing treatment is tantamount to violence."

The attended glared at the servant, tears in her eyes, but they ignored her and left. The guests near Mali looked at her with concern.

"In about, fifteen seconds," murmured Nova. She started to move from a sitting position to a crouch, tension in her legs.

Without a word, she spread her hand, showing five slender fingers.

Ix jolted up.

"You got a second?" he said.

All eyes locked on to him.

A beat later, lots of things happened, leaving no time in between.

With a sharp whistle, the shadow overhead grew stronger.

Nova disappeared from sight, and, at almost the exact same moment, the sound of bodies crashing together rang out behind Ix.

The fallen tarp temporarily obscured their vision. Screams resounded from across the courtyard.

The cloth had also covered Ix, but he was the first to see what was happening around him because he was standing. Hostages and captors alike were crouched on the ground, covering their heads in a reflexive attempt to protect themselves. A few of the servants were looking over at the pillar where the wand-wielding woman had been, their faces filled with shock. Even the bald man seemed taken aback, and he held his wand in front of him with his eyes closed.

Directly in line with the trajectory of the wand was Mali, lying on her back as if she'd been knocked backward.

It was almost as though a spell had been loosed from that wand.

What in the…?

Ix stared at the scene, dumbfounded.

The man waved his wand about furiously.

Ix immediately ran in that direction. He stumbled over someone and almost tripped.

The man noticed Ix closing in and let out a small scream. The tip of his wand fell squarely on Ix.

Ix raised his arm, but he would still need about three more steps to close in.

Just as he realized he wouldn't make it, a gray shadow descended into view. By the time it landed, the bald man was already knocked over. He wouldn't get up again.

"Are you all right?" asked Yuui, her wand trained on the man.

"That's the third time," replied Ix.

"What?"

Rain fell. It had grown stronger while Ix had been in the courtyard. He rubbed his eyes.

Ix walked over to the bald man, with Yuui behind him. He appeared to be unconscious. Ix picked up the stick that had fallen by the man's feet. It was a crude thing, just a stick that had been poorly carved to resemble a wand. Ix's evaluation of it didn't change now that he was seeing it up close.

He looked at Mali. Her attendant had wrapped her arms around the woman and was trying to sit her up. It seemed she was still alive. Ix then glanced to the opposite side of the courtyard to see Nova walking in his direction. The remaining servants had thrown their sticks to the ground and were gradually moving away from her.

The sound of many footsteps approaching echoed from inside the building.

Everyone crouching down seemed to realize what was going on; slowly, they began to stand and exchange relieved looks with their neighbors.

"Wh-why—?!"

An unsteady shout rang across the courtyard.

One of the guests was pointing in Ix's direction. Their entire body was quivering from fear or rage.

Confused, Ix looked to his side.

He saw Yuui's frozen expression.

Her face was visible.

8

After they were taken back to the room on the second floor, quite some time passed. The chaos on the floor below seemed to have calmed significantly—perhaps most of the guests had already gone home.

While they waited, Elion poked his head in, asked them to wait just a little longer, and took Ottou away with him. It was already midnight. The rain was slowing down, but it felt damp where they were.

Ix and Yuui sat in chairs side by side, but they didn't speak.

He was fiddling with the stick he'd picked up earlier.

Something was bugging him.

Not something about the stick, but what it had caused him to remember.

The door clicked open, and Nova returned to the room. She headed over to Yuui and sat across from her. Just as Ix had changed, she was now back in her normal baggy clothing. Ix had heard about her real job moments before.

"How's Mali?" he asked hesitantly.

"She's not, in good condition," replied Nova evenly. "She can speak, but she is worse than before. It may not be today or tomorrow, but she doesn't have long left."

"Oh no…"

"I was told there are three reasons for her decline: the late administration of her medicine, the strain of being kept in the courtyard for a long time, and emotional stress." Nova's bangs rustled as her eyes shifted to Yuui. "If she had been held captive any longer, she would be in an even worse state. They expressed their thanks to you, Yuui."

Ix glanced at the stick in his hands, and Nova continued.

"You must have been mistaken, when you thought you saw a spell. Her attendant said Mali fell, because she slipped."

"…Uh-huh."

"They did not tell me, anything else."

After that point, the guards had burst in and captured the attackers. Only two of the interlopers had been armed, both of whom Yuui and Nova brought down. The rest immediately surrendered when the guards had trained their wands on them.

In the end, Ix still didn't know who those people were or what their goal was. When he mentioned that, Nova cocked her head and said, "This is just, my guess, but..."

"You figured it out?" said Ix.

"Based on their message, I think they were an extremist group from the Secession Sect. Do you know of them?"

"Vaguely."

Within the New Order denomination of Marayism were a number of sects. Some of the most prominent ones included the Reformation Sect, who aimed to reform the Church from within; the Secession Sect, who pushed for independence; and the Balance Sect, who took on portions of the other two groups' ideologies.

"The Secession Sect, wishes to expand the New Order's influence, even if it means using force," explained Nova. "I heard, when I visited the church, that some extremist groups within the sect, were planning to use the Feast of Meat to start a revolt."

"They wanted to use a festival...?" asked Ix.

"Yes," she replied flatly. "There are a few examples, of people becoming worked up at festivals, shouting anti-war or anti-country opinions, to the point where it led to a revolt. It seems they planned to start that, on purpose. I have heard they plotted, to incite the people and to destroy the Feast of Meat, because it doesn't align with New Order ideals. This was believed to be too difficult, though, as there are few extremist groups, even within the Secession Sect."

"Did they go after this banquet because that other plan seemed impossible?"

"It was, out of desperation."

"Which is why their plan was so ridiculous," said Ix with a shake of his head. "But you know a lot, don't you? Guess you'd need info like that with the job you've got."

"Correct."

Yuui wore her typical expression as she listened to them speak. After people had glimpsed face and skin, she'd quickly regained her composure and responded calmly. Thanks in part to Elion's skillful cover-up, the attendees didn't blame her on the spot. Still, she was subjected to horrible things from them. Some even shouted that they were certain she was the culprit. The Obryle family would likely shoulder some of the blame from this incident as well. She just hoped it wouldn't lead to anything bad happening to Ottou...

When Ix and Nova's conversation came to a lull, Yuui made a suggestion.

"Let's go with Gidens to Notswoll tomorrow."

"All right," said Ix, nodding.

"The Feast of Meat is the day after, yes? It is unfortunate I won't be able to see the festival in Leirest, though," said Yuui.

"Did you want to see it?" he asked.

"Well, not particularly... Though, yes, I did notice those large wooden figures being built. I was somewhat curious as to their use."

"The parade," clarified Nova. "They walk the figures down, the main road. It is a normal display in many big cities."

"Ah, is that so?"

Ix's eyes opened wide. He stared at his palms.

"That's it...," he said.

"Hmm?" Yuui blinked, not understanding.

"I started it...," he muttered. "That's why I couldn't remember it; it was just a stick..."

"By 'just a stick,' do you mean that one?" asked Nova as she pointed to the one in his hands.

"Hmm? No, it's got nothing to do with this. If I'm right, that one's in at the shop still... Yeah, I'm sure I put it in Morna's storage."

Yuui stared into his face straight on.

"Um, could you please start over from the beginning and explain things so we can all understand? This is such a bad habit of yours," she grumbled.

"From the beginning...," he said, frowning. "Well... Right, it's

Notswoll. I told you I remembered hearing the name somewhere, right? I just realized where."

"And that was?"

"We got an order from someone in that village a long time ago."

Ix sighed before continuing.

"Engraved number: 3403, Passing. It was the first thing I ever made. Or the first I was supposed to make."

CHAPTER 3 ◄──── The Witch Lives

1

Ix was sitting backward. The walls of the wagon obstructed his views of the scenery ahead of and beside him. To make matters worse, all he could see out the back was a continuous stretch of rural land, which wasn't particularly interesting, either. He resigned himself to staring at the ruts its wheels were gouging into the ground.

The road was entirely unworked and now muddy from the rain, so the pair of old bulls in front of the wagon were struggling to haul it. They gasped for breath when they moved off the paved road and started to climb a hill. By contrast, the farmer steering the bulls seemed entirely composed. His head, topped with close-shaven white hair, was locked on the path ahead the entire time. The old man was quiet. He never said anything, and his only response to questions was a shake or nod of his head. His tanned skin, lined with deep wrinkles, spoke of his many years in this world.

Riding the wagon was uncomfortable, of course, but it was the odor coming from the large kegs piled in the wagon that Ix was really getting sick of. In the beginning, he'd thought the smell was nice, but it seemed disgusting now that he'd been inhaling it for the whole trip. Recently, it had started to mingle with the scent of the rain, creating a suffocating heaviness that left a tightness in his chest.

They had departed Leirest before the sun had shown its face. Leaving the city had taken a while, since the man inspecting them had gone back and forth between the guardhouse and the wagon countless times, perhaps out of exhaustion. The three of them, too, had barely slept because they hadn't left the Obryle mansion until past midnight. Not long after departing, Yuui started to nod off and eventually laid her head on Nova's shoulder to snooze. Nova seemed to have fallen asleep as well. They both leaned quietly against the wall of the wagon. To be honest, Ix couldn't be certain they were sleeping, since both their faces were concealed. Across from him sat Gidens, who was also out cold. Snores escaped from his half-open mouth, and there were still dark circles below his eyes.

The wagon came to a sudden halt, and Ix almost toppled over. He turned to look forward, thinking they'd dropped something in the road. The farmer hadn't changed position, but Ix could see the man gesturing in his direction with his chin.

He heard the squelch of footsteps in the mud. When the sound came around the side of the wagon, a woman moved into view. She was carrying a heavy-looking barrel. Her eyes met Ix's.

She looked older than him, perhaps even older than Morna. She had plain features, and her hair fell in gentle waves. While she was thin and of average height, *haggard* was perhaps a better description. Her outfit was made from simple cloth, over which she wore a plain apron. She looked like a maid who'd stepped out when she was in the middle of cooking, or maybe a housewife. Or she would have, had her feet not been coated in mud.

The woman glanced around the inside of the wagon and blinked in surprise. Taking care not to wake the sleeping passengers, she quietly loaded her barrel onto the cart. As she tried to climb in herself, her feet slipped on the muddy ground.

Ix quickly reached out to grab her shoulder, just managing to make it in time. A moment later and she would have cracked her forehead on the wagon.

"Th-thank you," she said.

He offered her a hand up, which she took with her own rough palm. Once in the wagon, she sat like Ix, facing backward, her feet dangling over the edge. They started moving again right after that.

"Um, so…," she said as she looked over hesitantly toward Ix and parted the bangs plastered to her forehead by the rain. Quietly, she asked, "Are you friends of Gidens? Or Gramps?"

"Gidens," replied Ix.

"Where are you coming from?"

"Leirest."

"You came all the way out here from the big city? Do you have some business in town? Wait, don't answer. Let me guess. Hmm…"

She crossed her arms, gazed upward, and sat silently like that for a while.

"I'll just tell you," said Ix.

"No, wait, wait! Just a little longer, okay?"

"…All right." Ix nodded, relenting for some reason.

He was surprised he'd obeyed her. All he could think was that his body had naturally gone along with what she said. He really had intended on ignoring her protest and telling her…

She hemmed and hawed for a few more moments, then held up a finger.

"I got it; you've come to see the festival!"

"…Yeah, that's about it."

"Oh, really? Ha-ha… That's a bit odd." Her eyes widened.

"Is it?"

"Yeah. People come from the villages nearby, but all the people who live in towns near Leirest just go there. I mean, our little hamlet's festival doesn't hold a candle to the one in that huge city, right?"

Just before he could ask her about the festival, she let out a small cry.

"We're almost in the village."

She was pointing to a square white stone placed off to the side of the road in a meadow. It was half buried by tall weeds. Perhaps it was

a marker to show the border of the village? Or maybe a magic beast deterrent? It faded from view while Ix lost himself in thought.

Getting to his knees, he strained forward to glimpse houses built here and there throughout the fields. The village was larger than he'd imagined and, just as he'd heard, it bordered an expansive forest.

Immediately after entering the village, they passed by a small house beside the road. The woman told him that was Gramps's house. He wasn't headed there now, though, as the storage he was going to load the cargo into was in the middle of the village.

But the cart stopped again before they got that far.

"Ah, this is me," she said, leaping off the wagon. "Sorry, could you help me get that down?"

The two of them lowered the barrel together. It was quite heavy and felt like it had liquid in it. He suspected she'd gone out on her own to get water.

Across the fields beside the road stood a large house. It was a bit extravagant for a farmer. It was the closest building to the forest, which at this distance seemed to press up against the back of the building. This was her home, apparently.

"Ah, thanks. Oh, I'm sorry, I didn't even ask your name," she said.

"Ix."

"Ix? The festival isn't until tomorrow. Do you have somewhere to stay?"

"Not yet."

"Ah-ha-ha, must be nice to be young and living life on a whim. Well then, you can try asking that sleepyhead," she said, pointing into the wagon. "Gidens'll probably do you a favor. If not, well... you're welcome to come stay at my place."

"You sure?"

"I don't recommend it. There's nothing in my house. Oh, that's not me trying to say no in a roundabout way; feel free to stop by... Hmm? What's wrong?"

"Uh, your name...?"

"Ah, I forgot to say? Sorry, I'm Camilla."

"Camilla?"

"It's actually pronounced Cah-mee-la, but either's good," she said with a smile. "It's such a strange name anyway."

"No, it's...," started Ix; then he hid his mouth with his hand and shook his head.

"It's so rare we get visitors from Leirest. Well, we might just see each other again soon, if you're unlucky!"

"W-wait," stammered Ix before he could think otherwise, stopping Camilla as she turned to go. "Uh, well..." He cast his eyes around the wagon. "Those kegs stacked over there... Do you know what's in them?"

"The kegs?"

"Yeah. I've been next to them since this morning; it's making me feel dizzy."

"Oh? Um, it's...oh, what was it called...?"

"Mead."

"Huh?" asked Ix without thinking as the response came in a coarse voice that didn't belong to her.

"It's mead." The voice belonged to the white-haired farmer, who was still facing forward as he repeated himself. "Tradition to drink it at the festival."

Ix almost asked the farmer why he hadn't spoken before now, though there probably wouldn't have been a response anyway.

2

The wagon continued on for a short while.

Everywhere Ix looked, there were fields. Few people were working them, however, perhaps on account of the rain. A handful of villagers looked up at the wagon as it passed nearby, but they quickly lost interest and went back to their farming.

It was harvest season, and there was nothing left growing in most of the fields. Some still had crops, but Ix couldn't tell if they hadn't been harvested or just weren't in season yet.

Finally, they arrived in an area with several buildings clustered together. The ground had been smoothed flat to form a sort of rudimentary village square. The bulls came to a rest right there. Ix hadn't seen the farmer bid them to halt, but this seemed like a good place to do so.

The farmer opened the door of the nearest building. There were racks and stacked kegs lining the walls, as well as scattered tools needed for farming. Ix couldn't see deep into the building, since it was dark, but it was clearly not a place suitable for dwelling. It was some sort of storage unit.

"…Hmm?" Gidens half opened his eyes. He looked to either side and let out a huge yawn. "Aaaah, ladies, we've arrived."

At his call, Yuui and Nova raised their heads. They'd been dead asleep.

Even during that, the farmer had been going about his work. He climbed up into the wagon, and Ix and the other three decided to help him.

They moved the cargo into the building, which seemed to consist entirely of goods from Leirest. There was a wide variety of things, from edibles, such as preserved foods and spices, to everyday objects, like iron tools and candles. They must have taken what they produced in the village to Leirest to sell, then gathered what they needed in Leirest to bring back here.

But those kegs were proving troublesome. They were so heavy that Ix couldn't lift a single one on his own. A few of them worked together to lower them from the wagon, where the farmer would take them. He then rolled them on their side into the storage building.

There were a lot of other piles of smaller goods, which required numerous trips between the wagon and storage.

Ix had thought it was storage for farming equipment, but near the entrance, there was a wooden box containing brightly painted wooden sculptures, flutes, drums, and other similar objects. Ix bent over to take a quick look at them.

"Things for the festival," said Gidens when he noticed Ix. He was holding a bottle in one hand. "Tomorrow's going to be loads of fun."

"You like music?" asked Ix.

"Hey now, I'm no kid. The Feast of Meat's a day for eating all the meat and drinking all the alcohol you want. I am looking forward to it, yessir."

That wasn't the kind of thing you'd expect to hear from an upstanding member of the Marayist clergy. Maybe the rules granted exceptions to readers.

Just then, a new voice came from the doorway.

"Aw, and here I came to help out..." Looking into the building was a heavyset man. Ix couldn't discern his features, since he was backlit. "You already all finished up?"

"Take a look," said Gidens, his arms spread as he left the storage building.

"Well, darn. I was hoping to do a taste test while I was helping... Oh, and who are these folks?" asked the heavyset man.

"Travelers from Leirest. Guess they're interested in seeing the festival here."

"Hmm? Some strange folks, then."

"My name is Yuui," she said with a bow from near the entrance. Nova and Ix also introduced themselves and left the building.

The complete opposite of the rail-thin Gidens, even this man's arms and legs were broad. He was middle-aged, with thick layers of both muscle and fat on him. A magnificent beard sprouted from his chin. His eyes were narrow, making it look like he was always grinning slightly. His loud voice and the red cast to his face implied he'd been drinking.

"Ha-ha-ha, well, I'm not from round these parts, either," he said with an excessive guffaw. "The name's Gus. I'm from a nearby village, but I came over to help out with the celebration."

"Where he's from, cutting down the amount of alcohol before the festivities is considered helping," said Gidens with a shrug. "Your boy's probably crying."

"Oh, come now, it's a kind heart that lightens the load for others, even if just a bit. My boy's happy when I do. Mr. Priest, is it right for you to take issue with the kindness of others?"

"How many times do I have to say it? I'm not a priest. I'm a reader."

"Oh yeah, I remember now. Ha-ha-ha-ha!" Gus's tummy shook with laughter. "I'm just going to pop in there. Some cargo I want to inspect."

Looking up, Ix noticed other villagers had gathered around as well. Mostly young people and children who had nothing else to do. It seemed many of them had come from nearby villages to help, like Gus. There would likely be even more the next day.

The bystanders pressed in closer to Ix, overflowing with curiosity at seeing someone new and getting a bit carried away by the excitement of the upcoming festival. Ix looked for Yuui and Nova and saw them casually extract themselves from the crowd to watch from the side.

"Did you really come from Leirest?" asked one of the onlookers.

"Yeah," replied Ix.

"Ooh, are you a merchant?"

"I'm an apprentice wandmaker."

"Look what we got here, a big, scary, murder weapon–making craftsman!"

The crowd buzzed. Ix didn't sense any derision or offense from them. It was more like they were welcoming him in their own way, though this still didn't exactly make Ix feel comfortable.

While the onlookers made a ruckus, the farmer wordlessly gathered his cargo and loaded it into the wagon again. He pulled on the reins and turned to go back down the road they'd come up. As he left, people called, "Bye, Gramps!" or "Thanks again!" Ix also tried to express his gratitude, but he wasn't sure if the man heard him or not.

"Gramps doesn't talk," said a short child who'd come out of the storage building. She sounded mature for her age.

"He does," insisted Ix.

"But no one's ever heard him speak."

"Is he your grandpa, little girl?"

"I'm not a little girl—I'm Yonda."

"Is he your grandpa, Yonda?"

"He's not anyone's grandpa. Everyone just calls him that."

"Uh-huh."

"Hey," said Yonda as she tugged on his sleeve and pointed toward Yuui and Nova. "Why is that lady over there hiding her face?"

"She's got a reason for not wanting anyone to see it."

"Hmm… Have you seen it?"

"Yeah."

"What kind of face does she have?"

"A normal one."

"Then why's she hiding it? Will she show me if I ask her to?"

"Hmm, I'm not so sure."

"Why not?"

"She's taller than you." Ix crouched down and whispered, "More importantly, I've heard Gramps talk."

"Huh? When?" Yonda blinked in surprise.

"Just a bit ago."

"What'd he say?"

"'*Mead*.'"

Ix followed the stream of young people and found himself at a spacious building that appeared to be a meeting hall. Beside the structure was a sturdily built well house. Inside was a simple fireplace built into the wall, where a large pot had been set over a flame. A man with sleepy eyes stared at the steam rising from the pot. A bunch of other things had been leaned up against the wall, and Ix was told they were food or other objects for the festival the next day.

Looking around, he noticed elderly villagers joining the youngsters in the group. They sat down in any old place. Not everyone could cram into the building, so a number of people were left standing outside and peering in. By now, Ix and the others were brushing up against the wall. Something was beginning.

"All right, let me just go and show you I'm not some two-bit reader, now," said Gidens as he passed nearby and grinned at them.

With a small but thick book in hand, Gidens moved to an open space in the center, which prompted a sudden outburst from the crowd as they began chattering away. He gently raised a hand to call for silence.

"Tomorrow's the festival," he said, just like he was chatting with friends. "No matter how many words of thanks I make y'all listen to, you'll just drink it all away and they'll slip outta your head. Least you could do is lend me an ear."

"Pretty rich for someone just reading from a book!" came a gibe from the crowd, and everyone laughed.

"Oh, so you saying you can read now?" shot back Gidens.

"Sure I can! You taught us, after all."

"Sorry to say, but what I taught you isn't enough to call reading." His expression was relaxed as he pushed back against the comments. "You done? No matter what wonderful teachings the Lord gives us, they ain't got no point if you don't understand what they mean. So then when you're making your list of things you're grateful for, I should come in second or third or maybe fourth place, 'cause I read you these teachings. Have some respect, folks."

"We will once you do something worth respecting," quipped someone else.

"Ha-ha, a great thing to say," said Gidens. He looked down for a moment and flipped quickly through the pages of his book. "All righty then, that is exactly what we're going to talk about today. What sorts of acts should you respect? And what does it mean to respect someone...?"

And so Gidens began to speak. His sermon was unconventional, just like it had started. The audience didn't listen in reverent silence. There was a constant string of insults and people pointing out things that didn't make sense in the teachings, and each time, Gidens would respond without missing a beat. This led to an unbroken stream of words. Gidens wasn't just reading. If a difficult part came up, he would explain using everyday examples that would draw laughter from the crowd.

Ix kept an eye on Nova's expression as she stood next to him. He couldn't tell where she was looking, but she was listening with rapt attention.

Gidens's sermon came to an end after about an hour.

The villagers left the meeting hall, jabbering away as they did. The youngsters who had been with them said their good-byes because they had other preparations to take care of. Only a few people remained.

Gidens walked up to them.

"Hey, so how was that? Was I impressive?"

"It was, good," replied Nova.

"There weren't any mistakes?" asked Ix.

"Not really. There was a problem, with the delivery, though," she said.

"Ha-ha, Miss Bangs, you've got a keen eye, don't you?" he said with a grin. "How 'bout you, Miss Hood?"

"I think you spoke well," replied Yuui.

"Keeping it simple? Ah, well, that's my job, then. Other than that, I just keep an eye on the villagers and do purifications or funerals if something happens. It's a pretty easygoing career."

"I'm wondering if I could ask you a favor," said Ix.

"That'll depend on what it is."

"It's our fault for coming all of a sudden, but we don't have any place to stay tonight. There anywhere you can recommend? We just need some walls and a roof over our head."

"Ah, hmm." Gidens folded his arms. He rubbed his stubbly chin with his palm and fell into thought for a moment.

"There's no space anywhere?" asked Ix.

"Well... I'm sure you could find space in a barn or somewhere, but I wouldn't recommend it." A furrow appeared between his brows. "It's only fall, but night and early mornings get pretty chilly. If you don't mind your fingers swelling up, then I'll show you the way, but you're a craftsman, right? And even then... I mean, you saw it before; there are loads of folks here from other towns filling up any place you might want to stay. If you were just one man, we could probably squeeze you in somewhere, but 'cause you've got the ladies, too..."

"Oh no, what are we going to do?" muttered Yuui.

"Well, if that's the case, we've got something else lined up," said Ix.

"Oh? Where's that?" asked Gidens.

"Camilla's house."

Yuui and Nova both looked at Ix in confusion while Gidens let out a loud cry of shock. The remaining people in the meeting hall all turned their eyes toward them.

Gidens waved to show them it was nothing, then circled an arm around Ix's shoulders. He steered him to a corner of the room, brought his stubbly face close to him, and lowered his voice.

"W-wait, you saying you're a friend of Camilla's?"

"Not a friend, but we talked earlier," replied Ix.

"Huh? Wh-when's 'earlier'?"

"On the way to the village. She got on the wagon on the way back from fetching water."

"Oh...," he choked out. "Why didn't you wake me when she climbed in?"

"You were sleeping."

"…Okay, then how'd you end up talking 'bout staying at her place?"

"How…? She just said to ask you about accommodations, but if you had nowhere we could stay, then we could go to her house. She just invited us."

Gidens looked resigned as he removed his arm from Ix's shoulders. He turned to Yuui and Nova, who had been left behind, and said, "All right. Tonight, y'all will be staying at her place. But," he said with a serious expression, "I'm coming with you. You all right with that?"

"Hmm? I don't mind, of course," said Yuui with a nod despite her confusion.

"All righty, it's settled, then. I've got a meeting about tomorrow coming up, but I'll bring some dinner round once I'm done in the evening. Let Camilla know. No eating without me, you hear? I'm looking at you, Ix."

"I'm not that voracious," he deadpanned.

3

Before they went to Camilla's house, they decided to take a glance around the village. Or so they intended, but it was just fields as far as the eye could see, with nothing to really look at. Though the place was buzzing with preparations for the festival, it wouldn't seem like anything more than your average farming hamlet to people who'd lived in Leirest. The light rain from that morning was still falling.

The view was good because there was nothing to block it, so you could see the entire village no matter where you went.

They could now draw a simple map of Notswoll. First, there was the wide road running from the southeast to the northwest.

The wagon had come up from the southeast, which meant that was the direction Leirest lay in. The villagers seemed to treat that as the entrance to the village as well, probably since it was closest to the capital. The number of buildings steadily increased as you moved farther into town, with the most in the center. Their numbers dwindled again if you went to the northwest.

The forest was on the west side of the village. The fields in that area had uneven outlines as they ran across the edge of the woods. With the exception of Camilla's house, which Ix had seen on his way into town, no homes were built near the forest. Typically, you would assume that was to avoid any magic beasts that lurked in there, but things were different here. There was practically no division between the woods and the village, as though it was a part of the settlement itself.

Which meant they weren't staying away out of fear of magic beasts.

The group happened upon a townsperson leaving the fields. She was a woman in her fifties. Her face was wrinkled, but her body was muscular, and her skin was darkened by the sun. She stared openly at them.

"Hello," said Yuui in greeting. "We are the travelers who arrived this morning. We apologize for any fuss we've caused."

"Ah, so you're the curious lot come in from Leirest?" she replied in a roughened voice.

"Uh, yes, I suppose you could call us that..."

"Hmm..." The woman gazed at the three of them for a while. "You're just as strange-looking as I heard, too. Bangs, a hood, and a sourpuss. What sort of combination is that?"

"Oh, um, you could say it just sort of happened."

"Hmm. Well, tomorrow's festival got both townies and outsiders. You can just have fun. No one'll complain if you eat some food."

"Thank you." Yuui bowed her head, and Ix stepped forward.

"I want to ask you a question," he said.

"Oh, so it's Sourpuss up next. What is it, then?"

"Do you know anything about the witch?"

The woman's expression tensed the moment she heard the word *witch*. She forced a smile and glanced from side to side.

"You can't talk about it?" he asked.

"...I see," she said and let out a sigh. "Nah, it's not something you can't talk about, and I guess someone's got to tell you, since you're not from here. But...it's not exactly the kind of thing I want to bring up."

"We've got the gist already. She lives in the forest, has been alive for a few hundred years, sometimes eats people."

"That's plenty, then. You saying there's something else you want to know?"

"Twenty years ago," started Ix, fixing his gaze onto the woman, "there was apparently a baby from this village the witch ate. You know about that?"

The woman stared back at him, neither confirming nor denying.

Her arms tensed; she was clearly on edge.

"...I know 'bout it." She nodded slowly. "But not the details. Just that your information's a bit wrong."

"In what way?"

"It wasn't a baby from this village who was eaten. It was from somewhere else."

"What? From somewhere else? Where exactly?"

"That I couldn't tell you. You might not be aware, but twenty years back was when sonim was going round. Apparently, this pregnant lady caught it and was chased from her hometown. She wandered around until she eventually collapsed near the village. Someone here found her and brought her in."

"Wh-why?" asked Yuui, butting into the conversation. "Why would you take in someone so ill that they'd been chased from their home...?"

"Sonim was already all over this place. There were lots of folks with it here, and people were dropping dead every day. You saw it, didn't you? There are loads of youngsters and children here. The babies born after the sickness went away are finally growing up. So folks didn't really care at the time if there was one or two more sick people here. Obviously, some were against it, but the person who found the lady took care of her himself, so they let him be. And then the baby was born, but the mother died during childbirth. It was just around this time of year, too. It wasn't exactly the kind of situation where you'd throw a harvest festival, but we tried to do things right by holding a little worship. But then…*she* don't care about human things. She came that year, too, all the same."

The woman silently mouthed the word *witch*.

"Folks desperately protected their own children and family, but no one cared about a baby without anybody to look after them, no parent to raise them. A-and…" She stammered for words for a moment, then said, "Yeah, that little baby disappeared. That's all I can say. Y'all can go right on and have all the fun you want at the festival, but when the witch comes, you run as fast as you can. Not that I know if y'all are okay with being eaten."

"I'll make sure to remember," said Ix.

"That all you wanted to ask?" said the woman.

"Yeah, thanks."

"And what about you over there?" She gestured behind Ix. "We had Hood talk, then came Sourpuss, so is Bangs not going to step up and talk?"

"No," said Nova immediately with a shake of her head.

They tried talking to the other villagers they met after that but they only heard variations of the same story. They didn't receive any additional information. Whenever conversation turned to that baby, people suddenly struggled to find their words. Perhaps it was because the villagers all knew the three of them were outsiders, but they were always vague about the infant and would instead shift to telling obvious exaggerations, like how the witch had curved fangs or a forked tongue.

Granted, they didn't actually know what the witch looked like, so they couldn't rule those descriptions out entirely. But it did seem that the moment she appeared, everyone turned tail as fast as they could. There probably wasn't anyone who'd ever gotten a good look at her. All they knew was that she resembled a human figure draped in black. The key detail in all their stories was that the witch was "*really scary.*"

Even if they'd wanted to investigate the village further today, they couldn't, because there were no records on it. The majority of the populace couldn't read or write. Though the documents that Gidens had told them about did exist, those were stored far away in the parish church. If they went there now, they wouldn't be able to make it back in time for the festival.

They started thinking they should head to Camilla's house soon, and the three turned toward the village's southeast side.

As they walked, a sudden gale nearly blew back Yuui's hood.

"That was close...," she said as she quickly put it back in place. "But anyway, we haven't gleaned any particularly valuable information."

"We did learn something new," corrected Ix. "Don't know if it's valuable, though."

"And what is that?"

"No one's ever actually seen the witch eating someone."

"Uh, but..."

"Twenty years ago, someone only saw her snatch the baby away. Mali was also taken into the woods, but she wasn't devoured. She was told it might happen, so she ran away."

"Which means...what exactly?" asked Yuui with a frown.

"Not sure. That humans have to ripen, too? Maybe the witch likes people fattened up."

"...It seems our only choice is to wait for her to appear."

"That, or... This might be a bit obvious, but can't we just go into the forest?"

"Huh? I'm not sure. It doesn't seem off-limits..."

"That pair of adventurers met her, right? And that didn't have anything to do with the festival. This is just a hunch, but I bet they ran into her when they went off into the woods on their own."

"Which resulted in her threatening them."

"And that's weird, too..." Ix cocked his head in confusion. "I don't get what she was after with that at all. She handed them a bunch of enedo teeth and told them to turn the teeth in to the Guild? What would that have done?"

"It would ruin, the price," pointed out Nova.

"There is that," acknowledged Ix, "but I don't see why she'd suddenly get interested in everyday things. Like, she eats people, and nothing about that makes sense, which actually makes me sort of accept it. But with the enedo teeth thing, I can half understand it, which actually means I get it even less... Uh, I said something really contradictory just now, didn't I?"

"I hear what you're trying to say," said Yuui with a nod. "The contradiction, or perhaps confusion, comes from the fact that we are unsure of how to comprehend the witch, how to define her. Is she some mysterious being we can't possibly fathom? Or is she nothing more than a powerful magic-using human? These two understandings are mixed together. But this is exactly why meeting her..."

Their conversation continued. Eventually they heard a voice calling from behind for them to wait.

Turning around, they saw the man they'd met earlier, Gus, one hand raised as he approached. The group stopped walking and waited for him to reach them.

"Lookie there, it's you three," he said when he was close. "You're heading toward the city; does that mean you're already fed up with this boring town?"

"No, that's not it," said Yuui as she waved her hand.

"Well, that's good to hear. Anyway, Gidens was skulking around the food for the festival earlier; you wouldn't know what that was about, would you?"

"Oh, that's most likely—"

"Of course, it's for the guests. No, I didn't come here to give you a hard time about that. I kind of like y'all anyway, and I just went with the flow. That's not what I'm here about..." He lowered his voice and continued. "I heard y'all are going to stay at Camilla's place tonight. That true?"

"That's the plan," replied Ix.

"Really...?" Gus's eyebrows curved in distress, and he rubbed his left arm with his right hand a few times.

"Is there, a problem?" asked Nova, her head tilted.

"No... I wouldn't say that," he said, his tone turning hesitant in a way that didn't seem to fit his size. "It's just... Guess I feel like I should tell you that she's, how should I put it? You'll probably think this is absurd..."

After a moment of searching for the right way of putting it, he finally seemed to gather himself and continued.

"She's...cursed."

"Huh?" Ix couldn't stop the sound coming from his mouth.

"It's just... Her family passed when she was a little girl; she's lost most of her belongings and land, and there's this rumor that she brings young men from nearby villages to her home and, um, provides services. And everyone says the reason is because she's cursed by the witch."

"Wait a moment. Reason? Reason for what?" asked Yuui.

"Losing her family. The reason she's had so much bad luck, starting with that, anyway. You seen her house, yeah? That's the only home built that close to the forest. Maybe it's that, or maybe it's 'cause she apparently went to the witch's house in the woods a few times when she was a kid. That's when she got hexed...or so I've heard. And that's why, you know, people in the village keep their distance from her. They don't give her a hard time, mind you, but they won't go out of their way to interact with her, either. Gidens strikes up conversations with her, but he's a man of the cloth..."

"So you came by to warn us?" asked Ix with a crease in his brow.

"W-well, I'm just saying those are the rumors. Y-y'all have a nice one now."

He pulled his head in like he was embarrassed and went back up the road.

Well, regardless of who Camilla was, she had nothing to do with them, as they were just staying the night. And this superstition about a curse…they wanted to just brush that off, but for all they knew, the witch could have indeed used some unknown magic on her. There were more things to think about now.

They started walking down the road again, and Yuui asked Ix, "What sort of person was this Camilla? I mean, was she—?"

"I've never talked to a cursed person before, so I wouldn't know."

"Yes, I would imagine not."

"Besides," said Ix as he pointed in the direction they were headed, "it would be faster for you to just meet her yourself."

4

"Oh dear, I didn't realize there were two ladies. It won't be a very pleasant stay, but you're young, so I'm sure you'll manage," said Camilla.

"I-it's fine," said Yuui, so thrown off-balance that her vague response barely came out.

"Oh, so you won't be taking that hood off inside? Is there a reason for that?"

"Uh, yes…"

"Ooooh, so mysterious. Ah, I'm sorry, Yuui. I'm being so insensitive."

"No, it's—"

"And, Nova, you really don't talk, do you?"

"No," replied Nova.

"'*No*,' ha-ha… Ah well, nothing wrong with being direct."

Camilla was cheerful as she greeted them. She was currently showing them around the house. It was all built on one floor but had numerous rooms. It was probably the largest house in the whole village. Yuui had to try hard to hide her surprise.

Her surprise was not at the estate's…extravagance.

It was because there was absolutely nothing inside the mansion. Well, *nothing* was somewhat of an exaggeration. The first room as they entered the front door had a small square table and two chairs.

But that was it. There was nothing else.

None of the rooms they went into had any furniture. There were no daily necessities. There was literally nothing besides the floor, walls, and ceiling. It was hard to believe anyone lived there. Even if it was a house whose residents had moved out, you would expect to see a few more signs of life.

It was so bad, Yuui started to wonder if this woman was actually a real living, breathing human being.

Camilla showed Yuui to a room she said she could use, but it naturally had nothing in it. It was the one farthest from the front entrance, and the branches of the trees in the forest could be seen waving outside the window. The howling wind made an unpleasant noise.

"I don't get visitors, so I don't have any beds. Sorry about that. It's kind of like camping, though, just with a roof and walls. They don't leak, at least," said Camilla.

"Thank you for this," said Yuui.

"Thank, you," said Nova.

Compared to the wagon from the morning, this was a paradise. They had no reason to complain. What Yuui wanted to discuss was a different issue.

There came the sound of footsteps approaching the room, followed by Ix opening the door.

"Camilla, I wanted to ask you—"

"Don't enter a lady's room without checking first!" she shouted, cutting him off. "And I thought I said we could talk later. Wait just a little longer."

"...Okay."

With a mix of emotions on his face, Ix closed the door and left. Normally, he would have protested a bit more, but for some reason, he obeyed her immediately. That shocked Yuui; she wondered if he just wasn't good at dealing with personalities like Camilla's.

But why was this place so strange...?

Even if she'd lost her family and her belongings, it wouldn't be this bad. She might have sold her furniture and daily necessities, but there would be some things that wouldn't go. Disposing of them would take effort, so there really should have been more than just a table and two chairs.

They went back to the room with the only furnishings, spread a cloth on the floor, and sat down.

"Ummm, so then...," said Camilla as she sat facing them. "Guess we can start with what Ix wants to talk about. I just hope I can answer your questions."

"Before that, I want to confirm one thing," he stated, looking down at her because he was still standing.

"Go ahead, though it doesn't have to be just one. Two or three is fine, too."

"Is your full name Camilla Toah? And your father's name was Doen Toah?"

She tilted her head, grinning as she asked, "Did I tell you all that?"

"And a long time ago, you placed an order with Munzil Alreff."

"......" Camilla blinked many times, then slowly asked, "Who are you?"

"I'm Munzil's apprentice."

"...Is that so?"

"Fifteen, no, fourteen years ago," started Ix, gazing seriously at her, "a man named Doen came to Master's shop and ordered a staff. He'd requested one to give to his daughter, Camilla, who lived in Notswoll. They discussed the staff's specifications, and the order was placed that day. It was planned to be finished in six months. Doen said he'd bring his daughter along when he came to pick it up and left. A month later, a letter canceling the order came from Notswoll."

"You have a good memory," she said, impressed. "And here I am forgetting all sorts of things."

"It only came back to me recently," clarified Ix. "We got some good materials for the order, the reneel for the wood and the eshi amber for the core. They're not top-tier, but they should've made a good staff. For a while, I wondered why it was canceled so suddenly... I couldn't get over it. It was so long ago that I eventually forgot about it, though."

"Oh... So you're a craftsman, Ix?"

"I'm not; I'm just an apprentice."

"But still, a craftsman's apprentice... But if that's the case, I guess I do owe you an explanation. I caused so much trouble." Camilla gave a worried smile. "Mm, you've probably guessed it. Mom and Dad died. They got sick out of the blue... It wasn't sonim, though. The pandemic had ended a couple of years prior; this was just your average fever. I realized they had a high temperature in the middle of the night, and by morning, they were cold. I was so shocked..." She stared up at the ceiling for a moment. "Then, after they died, people from the village and other places came to the house in droves. They told me they'd lent my parents money or they'd had this agreement, and they took away all the things in the house. I was so shaken up by their deaths that I didn't even understand what was happening. I don't really remember it that well even now...

"One day, I was just sitting alone in a room, doing nothing in particular, and I remembered: *Ah, that's right, we ordered a staff.*

I'm not sure why that of all things came to me, because there was a lot of other important stuff going on... That's why I wrote that letter, gave it to Gramps, and had him deliver it to Munzil's shop. I really am sorry I didn't need the staff in the end."

"I see...," murmured Ix with folded arms.

A heavy silence descended on the room.

Yuui sat looking down in thought.

Wands and staffs were valuable items. Even if someone got one, they would need specialized education before they could use magic to its fullest. From the looks of this house, it was obvious that Camilla's parents had been wealthy. Despite that, the income of a landowner in a rural location wouldn't have amounted to that much at the end of the day. Buying a staff to give their daughter... that must have been a huge decision on her parents' part. And from Munzil, even, the greatest craftsman in the kingdom.

And yet, that hope had disappeared so quickly, lost along with her parents.

"But don't all look so glum, will you?" said Camilla as she stood and clapped her hands together. "Besides, this sort of thing happens everywhere. It was more than ten years ago, and I won't get anywhere by wallowing in pain and sorrow. I'm not young enough for that anymore. Cheer up, everyone. Tomorrow's the big festival, after all."

"Y-you say that, but...," said Yuui, bunching up her shoulders.

"Come on now, hmm... I know, Ix, smile!"

"Uh, what?" His eyes widened when he was suddenly mentioned.

"Smile! Like this, bring up the corners of your mouth. See, like this!" Camilla pushed up the edges of her lips with her fingers. "Should I do it for you?"

Ix's face tensed as he watched her digits come closer.

"N-no, f-fine, I'll smile," he said.

"That's a good craftsman!"

"I told you, I'm not a craftsman..."

Ix forced his expression to change with a stiffness that should come along with the squeaking of an unoiled hinge. He wasn't used to grinning. The more he tried, the less it resembled a smile, until at last, he seemed like a criminal about to be handed a death sentence. Camilla cried, "What is that?!" and held her sides as she chortled. Yuui felt bad, but she couldn't hold back her own laughter, either. The only one who didn't really react was Nova.

That's when the front door opened, and a man stepped in with a "pardon the interruption."

"Ah, welcome," said Camilla with a wide smile.

"H-how's it going, Camilla? I grabbed some food." Gidens seemed somewhat shaken, as his eyes wouldn't stay still.

"Wooow, that's so much! Thank you—it'll be like we're having our own early Feast of Meat tonight."

"Y-yeah… Well, I had some of the youngins get it together for me. Uh… B-but that's not important. Ix. You look like you're doing something strange." His roving eyes came to settle on Ix, who was in the corner of the room. "I mean…you are doing something strange; that's not what I mean… What I mean is, what the heck are you doing?"

5

They ate a slightly early dinner. They sat in a circle on the floor, with the food Gidens had brought in the center. Most of it had been prepared the day before, or several days prior, and was strongly seasoned. A few of the items hadn't been spiced yet, however.

"Not much I can do about the grub; the kids just sort of grabbed random stuff," said Gidens. "Don't worry about that, though—tomorrow's going to be amazing. We've got a tradition where they slaughter a head of cattle. It gets butchered, roasted up, then eaten right there in the village square."

"That's quite a treat," said Yuui with a nod, sounding impressed. "What other events will there be?"

"There's not really anything you could call an event. Basically, start eating and drinking in the morning, then there's the music and the dancing... Then the boys and girls disappear."

"...Camilla, is there anything you recommend?"

"Uuuh, well, I don't go to the festival, so I can't really say."

"Oh, I-I'm sorry..."

"Don't apologize. I don't mind at all."

Despite her saying that, an uncomfortable tension choked the room.

"Ah, and then...," said Gidens as he raised an arm and tried to clear the air. "At the end of the festival, when night falls, they light a big fire, and people dance in the fields."

"That's, unusual," murmured Nova, who hadn't spoken yet.

"Ha, I don't think it's as unusual as Miss Bangs speaking," teased Gidens.

"Dancing occurs in many locations, but there are no places where it falls traditionally, at the end, not that I've heard of, anyway. Why does it come last?" asked Nova.

"Why...? Thought I told you. 'Cause that's when *she* comes, and that's when it's all over, even if we don't want it to be."

"The, witch?"

"That's the one."

"I knew people thought of her that way," said Camilla with a frown. "In my opinion, it's all a big misunderstanding."

"Oh look, Camilla's talking about the witch," groused Gidens.

"Don't make fun," she retorted.

"Camilla, do you know the witch?" asked Yuui, her head tilted.

"You could say I know her, but that was a long time ago," said Camilla with a vague smile.

"These folks are researching her. You should tell them about her," said Gidens.

"Oh, is that so? Hmm, even if you'd asked me, it was so far back…"

Ix recalled the stories about Camilla losing her family due to the witch's curse. He obviously thought this was absurd, but the woman herself didn't seem to mind at all.

Gidens got the conversation back on track by saying, "But anyway, tradition has it that only the young, unmarried folks who live in the village can go into the fields. The adults' job is to keep the beat from the edges. There are a ton of youngsters this year, so it'll be real lively. Unfortunately, you folks'll only be able to watch from the outside."

"…That's, odd," remarked Nova in a tone that didn't sound like she thought it was strange at all. "This tradition doesn't seem based in Marayist teachings, at all."

"There ain't nothing strange about it." Gidens gave a frustrated smile. "Not like people are going to do each and every little thing perfectly in line with the teachings. Besides, scripture ain't actually taught properly out in the country. Makes sense to me that each place would have their own unique traditions."

"Yes, you may be right."

"And here, it serves another purpose, too. It's not really a tradition, just a chance for people to find someone they might want to marry. When they run from the witch, they'll grab the arms of a person she's after and pull them away. Lost so many youngsters in that war a while back that it's life-and-death for communities like these. We'll have problems if they're swept away by outsiders. But…" Gidens looked at each of them in turn. "I don't think we've got to worry 'bout that with you three."

"Gidens, don't be rude," said Camilla in a chiding tone. "I'm sorry, everyone. I swear, he didn't used to be like this."

"You've known each other a long time?" asked Ix.

"Yeah. I was just a girl when I moved to the village. Back then, Gidens was a, hmm, a sort of pleasant, silver-tongued young man. I wonder what happened…"

"He seems to have changed quite a lot since then," mused Yuui as she looked at his and Camilla's faces.

"Don't talk about that time. Some people want to forget their past," Gidens grumbled.

"Oh, let's keep going, then," said Camilla happily as she brought her hands together. "I do miss it. What would you call— your fire? Delivering the scriptures to the villagers, reading this and that, saying such and such is the right teaching. Folks seemed real fed up with you."

"I was a fool."

"So that means when you grow wise, you get better at glossing over things than you do at actually following the teachings?"

"Hmph, can't go around spouting inconsistent interpretations of the scriptures. If only they'd get it together and put out a unified opinion, but there's so much arguing going on inside the Church that they're missing the point."

"I, agree." Nova nodded.

"Y-you do, now…? Miss Bangs, you're really digging in, ain't ya?"

"Well, everyone seems to enjoy your sermons now, so I guess that's good. I kind of liked the you from those days, though," said Camilla as she closed her eyes and reminisced.

Gidens snorted. "I might have been green back then, but you were *naive*. Every day you'd be saying, '*I'm going to be a magic user; I'm going to be a magic user.*' You just followed me around all over the place."

"Ah-ha-ha, how old was I then?" Camilla gave a hearty chuckle. "It was because you told me about stuff outside the village. You were the only one who did that, with Gramps the way he is anyway."

"Ah, Gramps… How old is that man? I don't even know his name."

"Neither do I. Seems like he's been carrying things to and from the village forever."

Having known each other for so long, Gidens and Camilla's back-and-forth continued like an unbroken stream. Gidens was supposedly quite a bit older than Camilla, but you couldn't feel a difference in their ages as they chatted.

When the food had nearly disappeared, Gidens gave a grin.

"All right, time to bring out the pièce de résistance," he said.

"What's this?" asked Camilla with her head tilted.

"Ha-ha, I took the liberty of getting something special," he said.

He then drew a green package from his inner pocket. It looked like a small parcel wrapped in long green leaves and tied with cord. When he undid the cord, it released a fragrant smell and revealed thinly sliced meat.

"Worked real hard to pinch some of this stuff," he stated proudly. "It's meat, slow-roasted for an entire day. But you know what, it's even better when it's only half cooked. Trust me, I've tasted both."

"Won't they be angry at you later?" asked Yuui with an exasperated tone.

"No one has to know about it. The only people who're aware are the children I had bring it to me. They won't ever tell a soul."

Still, it seemed that he hadn't been able to sneak away a large amount, instead only managing to get five pieces, exactly enough for one each. Ix picked up a slice and looked at it. He brought it near his face and could smell a faint fruity scent.

"It's so delicious," said Yuui, the first to eat the meat. "What seasonings were used?"

"Well, there's—"

Gidens tried to answer, but the next person to take a bite was Nova, who then shouted in a voice louder than any they'd heard her use before.

"Yuui, spit it out!"

"Huh?" said Gidens, his brow furrowed.

"There's mewmose powder on it."

Nova walked briskly over to Yuui, took her hand, and made her stand up. She dragged her to the front door as she shoved her fingers into the girl's mouth.

"Ah, but, Nova—"

"It might be difficult by yourself, so I'll assist."

"But is mewmose—?"

"If I'm wrong, you can have my share. Just hack it up."

"O-okay, all right—"

The door opened, and the two disappeared outside.

The other three sat in confusion, staring at one another. No one else had brought the meat to their mouths yet.

"…She did say '*mewmose*,' didn't she?" muttered Gidens.

"That is what she said, yes," confirmed Ix, nodding.

With a crease between his eyebrows, Gidens touched the tip of his tongue to the meat and let out a groan. "Yeah, it feels numb now. The seasoning's so strong, I wouldn't've noticed if she hadn't said anything."

"…Do you have an antidote?" asked Ix, looking at the other two.

"There's none in the house," said Camilla, looking grim.

"Sorry, but I don't think something as rare as that'll be in the village." Gidens frowned. "But maybe there's someone who's got it. I feel like we bought some, though it was a while back."

Mewmose was the name of a poisonous plant. It could be recognized by its small yellow flowers and long, thin leaves, but it grew only in a tiny region in the south. Travelers and merchants occasionally carried their seeds, so it very rarely grew along the roads in other regions. Sometimes, you would find a magic beast who had mistakenly ingested it.

Consuming large quantities of the petals would kill you on the spot, but the symptoms of consuming small amounts were what it was famous for. It started with numbness in the tips of your toes and fingers. As time passed, you lost all mobility, after which you'd be unable to speak. You'd steadily lose the ability to move your own body until, eventually, you wouldn't even be able to breathe. There was an antidote for it, and you wouldn't succumb if you could take that, but if you waited until the symptoms progressed too far, then you could wind up with permanent disabilities.

One widely known story from history was that it took only a single meal laced with mewmose for a king to end up paralyzed. Afterward, the queen ruled through him, using him as her puppet. That was enough to make its danger well-known, so there weren't many people who accidentally ingested it. Thus, the antidote wasn't in wide circulation due to low demand, coupled with the difficulty of preparing it.

The front door opened again, and Nova came back with Yuui leaning on her.

"H-how is she?" asked Ix.

"She consumed only a small amount, and immediately threw it up, so I don't think it should be a big problem. For now, she should rest, and we should watch her condition," stated Nova calmly.

"Watch her condition? So what do we do if she develops symptoms?"

"Make her drink lots of water. That should be enough, to flush out small volumes of the poison."

"I-Ix, I'm fine, really…," Yuui managed with a strained smile. "Please excuse me—I'd like to go to my room. I will call if anything happens."

"Ah, s-sure," he replied.

Camilla opened the door for her, and she disappeared into the bedroom with a "good night."

Gidens stood and said, "Right, I'll be back in a bit. I'm going to ask round the village and see if anyone's got an antidote. And look into what happened with this food."

"I'll go, too," said Ix as he stood.

"Nope. If you come, no one's going to want to talk about anything, poison or no," said Gidens, turning him down.

Only the three of them remained in the room after that. Ix stared at the floor in thought.

The antidote… Would someone have some in the village? And why was there mewmose in the food for the festival anyway? Did someone add it by accident? It wasn't a plant that grew in this area. Could you really make a mistake like that?

Ix was even more worried about Yuui's condition. He'd heard that the tongue wasn't paralyzed until after the arms and legs, but there was no guarantee it couldn't happen in the opposite order. What if she was suffering, unable to cry out? Someone should stay by her side…

Just then, with a look of deep thought on her face, Camilla said, "The witch might…"

"Hmm?" asked Ix in response.

"Well, I was just thinking, the witch might have an antidote…" She pressed a hand over her mouth. "It's not just magic she's very knowledge about; she has a great command of medicine, too."

"Do…do you know where she lives?"

"I only went there when I was a kid…"

He looked out the window. There was still some light out. The forest was most likely dark already, but not so dark that they couldn't walk.

"Tell me how to get there," said Ix.

"But if you go now—"

"Please."

Ix's eyes bore into her, and she let out a groan. Eventually, she gave something like a sigh of resignation.

"All right. But I can't let you go alone. I'll show you the way," she conceded.

"You sure?"

"Yeah. And the conversation will go smoother if I'm there."

"Thanks." The moment he said it, he grabbed her arm and pulled her toward the door.

"Ah, w-wait!"

Just before they were about to step out the door, Ix turned back to Nova and said, "Stay by Yuui's side and keep an eye on her. Can you do that?"

"It is my duty, after all."

6

While she might have been resting in her room, Yuui wasn't tired yet. Nova had been staring at her the whole time, making her feel uncomfortable instead of sleepy.

She sat against the wall and waited for time to pass.

Camilla and Ix were on their way to see the witch. She hoped they wouldn't bump into her and get captured and eaten. Right now, it seemed like they were in greater peril than she was in for ingesting the poison, which made her even more anxious.

Eventually, she heard the front door open. Gidens had returned. He shook his head. There had been no antidote in the village.

"How you feeling? Anything strange happening?" he asked.

"I feel no different from usual," said Yuui lightly. "I'm sorry that your efforts were for naught..."

"Don't be—this is more important."

Just then, Nova politely interrupted their conversation and said, "Could you watch Yuui for a moment?"

"Hmm? I don't mind, but..." Gidens frowned. "What's this about? You still hungry?"

"No." Her face was expressionless as she shook her head. "I'm going to look outside."

"Outside?"

She didn't reply to Gidens's muttered question and left the room.

Now Yuui was left alone with him. They were silent, just as Yuui and Nova had been before, but Gidens seemed unable to relax. Every once in a while, he'd scratch his head and run his eyes around the room, here and there.

Yuui realized that she didn't feel too opposed to being alone in her room with a man at this hour. She smirked at the fact that she'd become so used to the culture of the kingdom.

"Ah, that's right…," said Gidens as he put his hand on his neck. "Sorry 'bout everything. Visitors like you are so rare, and then you had to end up dealing with all this."

"This isn't something you have to apologize for, Gidens." Yuui smiled, though she knew he couldn't see her face.

"Mm, I suppose so…" He shrugged. "And then you've got this dreary room… Though I guess it's not my place to be saying that, either…"

The two of them glanced around the area, which lacked anything beside their luggage. It was less dreary than empty. This wasn't the kind of place someone would live in.

"Are you…aware? Of why Camilla lives in a house like this?" asked Yuui. "She said the people from the village took the things inside, but surely that wouldn't result in this much empty space, no?"

Gidens didn't respond at all, almost like he hadn't even heard her speak. After a long moment of silence, he finally murmured something, as though talking to himself.

"…I don't know anything." He let out a heavy sigh. "Camilla… She's a good person."

"Yes, I can tell that about her."

"No, she's not just the average good person you'd think of. Sh-she's…" Gidens stammered for a moment. "She's never wanted anything for herself."

"I thought she wanted to become a magic user?"

"That was just a means, not an end. You know, miss, with the position I'm in, I read to the folks here. But while I might change how I say it sometimes, all scripture has the same meaning in the end. Yeah, you might want money, pretty women, and fun, but you should hold back those desires. Treasure the Lord and your neighbors and live a devout life. That's all it boils down to." He gave a sudden smile. "When I came to this town, I was filled with burning passion. I'd grab a villager and strike up a conversation with them and check up on every one of them individually. I'd go to them and ask, 'So what is it you're after? Ah, I see, now try and keep that greed in check.' I burned out a long time ago... But this one little girl, she said she wanted to help people."

"That girl was Camilla?"

"Her family was the richest in the village. I think she saw the suffering of the other townspeople and had her own thoughts about it... But when she told me that, I didn't have anything to say back. 'Cause that was exactly the kind of answer a virtuous person would give, just like the scriptures said. I talked to her so many times after that, but never once did she say she wanted something for herself."

"That is...moral."

"She's completely upright... Too upright, in fact."

"What do you mean by that?" Yuui raised her head.

"What? Did I offend you?"

"No...not particularly."

"Anyway, that was your pretty average goodness. Anyone could come up with something like that. But it's possible to go too far with normal, to stretch it out until things go wrong." His mouth curved at the irony. "...I thought she was just acting like a good little girl, so I tried all sorts of things to get her to say what she really wanted. I stuck at it, and eventually she told me she wanted to be a magic user. I thought, ah, she's finally said something selfish, but it wasn't anything. She just wanted to help people *using magic*. She might've even just said it 'cause I was bugging her about this and that, and I'd gotten annoying.

"I happily told her that being a magic user wasn't a proper life, but the more we talked about it, the more serious she got, until she wanted it with every fiber of her being. Her pops caved to her passion and promised to buy her a staff. But...then her parents died, and the villagers cleaned her out, and she..."

He stopped speaking there and adjusted his position on the floor. He looked over at Yuui with an unusually serious expression.

"Say, miss. Can you make Camilla a staff?" he asked.

"Why would you ask me?" questioned Yuui gently.

"I ain't got no money, and neither does she. But maybe if you asked that Ix to make one, just maybe…"

"I'm sorry, but I can't do that," she said firmly. "That would demean what craftsmen do. And it seems you may have come to the wrong conclusion; Ix and I don't have that sort of relationship. If you wish to ask him, it would be best for you to speak with him directly."

"…Ah. Yeah, you're right. That was rude of me. Sorry." He bowed his head.

Silence filled the room again.

Nova still hadn't returned. She'd said she was going to look outside, but how far was she planning to go? That seemed like a careless thing to do at night. Not that Yuui was in a position to worry over her…

"It was when Camilla…started throwing away the things in her house," remarked Gidens like he was talking to himself. "I came to the house more than once. I thought she might be thinking of dying… I was worried. When I asked her about it outright, she just laughed me off and said, '*I don't have any plans to.*' To this day, though, I can't shake the feeling she's just going to up and disappear eventually. But…" He looked down at the floor. "Sometimes, I think that would be better."

"Better for her to disappear?"

"I mean, you see what it's like. She's got nothing in this town…nothing."

Yuui started to say that wasn't true but stopped and closed her mouth.

She didn't think he was making a self-centered assumption, but she was a complete outsider. It would be irresponsible of her to object.

But it seemed that Gidens was well aware of this himself, as he jokingly said, "Well, that's just my personal opinion, and it's probably none of my business anyway."

7

Camilla walked with sure steps as she cut forward into the forest. To Ix, every direction looked exactly the same. If he got separated from her, he would probably be wandering the woods until he died. She reassured him a number of times that everything was okay. Her tone was calm, devoid of a single hint of panic.

"It's okay—the witch's house is just a little farther," she told him.

"...I've heard some rumors about her," he replied.

"Ah... Yeah, I've heard them, too. Everyone talks a lot of bull."

"You've met her before, right?"

"I didn't just meet her; I went there as a kid."

"Did you not know the rumors about her?"

"Nope, I knew. Maybe it was *because* I knew... Hmm, how do I put it...? It's not a big deal at all, but," she said in a cheery tone, "I actually had a little sister when I was young. She wasn't related by blood. Though I was the adopted one, not her. Anyway, she died in an accident."

"...An accident?"

"She was playing in the storehouse when she fell onto some farming equipment and got impaled. She bled so much. I was just outside, but by the time I noticed, it was too late."

"......"

"Come on, you could at least give me an 'uh-huh' so I know you're listening. It was so long ago, I barely even remember her name." She gave a stiff grin. "No one blamed me; in fact, they were actually all really considerate. A few years after that, I had this sudden idea. Don't know why it came to me so unexpectedly.

I thought, *If the witch eats people, maybe she can bring them back to life, too.* And so I went into the woods.

"Obviously, I got lost. I was scared and panicking, and I hurt myself... But that's when the witch appeared and saved me. She couldn't bring my sister back, but she treated my wounds. After that, I went to visit her at her house all the time. I mean, I didn't tell my parents about it, of course. At some point, I started thinking I wanted to be like her. That's why I asked for a staff. The witch seemed like an amazing magic user, so I wanted to be as incredible as she was... I had no idea how much a staff cost, but I was so, so happy when Dad said he'd purchase me one..."

"But—"

"Yeah... I stopped going to the witch's place a long time ago. Because...well, I don't have a staff. I'm nothing. There's not really any point in going now, you know? All I wanted was to help everyone... It's all I ever wanted."

Either the light rain that had been falling had slowed or the forest's trees were shielding them from the elements, because the forest was untouched. Every once in a while, a drop would fall from the leaves onto their heads or shoulders.

Their surroundings were dark, but Ix could still just about make out where he was stepping.

"Ix...," said Camilla.

"What?"

"You seemed like you really wanted to ask me about my staff. If that was fourteen or fifteen years ago, I would've thought you'd be just a little child...but you remember it really well."

"......"

"Oh, sorry. We don't have to talk about it if you don't want to."

After an internal debate, Ix said, "That was...supposed to be the first staff I ever made."

"Huh? How old were you?"

"Well, I wasn't going to craft it all by myself. I would have basically just ended up doing most of the carving. Up until then,

Master had never given me anything to do except little chores, but then he suddenly entrusted me with that. With making the staff." Ix thought back to those days. "I was surprised... But it was my first job. I carved it as he instructed, and he gave me harsh feedback the entire time. I managed to finish it, though. Master was going to take care of the rest, but that's when we got that letter."

"Oh, I've done something really terrible, haven't I?"

"It's not your fault."

"That's kind of you. But were you at least able to use that wood to make a different staff?"

"You can't do that." Ix shrugged. "When a craftsman produces a bespoke wand or staff, as opposed to a generic one, we seek out materials specific to that instrument. Once we decide on them, we can't use them for anything but that staff. That's even truer if the materials have been partially worked. That's why you don't normally hear about canceled orders. Unless the person who placed the order dies, we finish the product and demand payment, by force if necessary. That's also why we normally get full payment up front. Master was just a bit weird, though..."

"So then, what happened to the wood that was supposed to be my staff?"

"Didn't want to throw it away, so I stored it in the shop. I think it's buried somewhere in my fellow apprentice's store right now..."

"Oh my. I wish I had money; if I did, I would at least buy the materials from you."

The darkness in the forest steadily deepened. The sun shouldn't have completely set yet, but night fell early in the forest. Ix soon realized he couldn't even see a few paces ahead of himself. Camilla gripped his arm tightly. Blackness filled every crack and crevice of the woods, blotting out their vision.

In the middle of that darkness was a tiny white point.

They slowly drew toward it. There was nothing else for them to rely on. As they pressed on, their feet caught on roots of trees, and they almost tripped together. Once they'd approached the white speck, they realized what it really was.

It wasn't actually white; it was red. And it wasn't a point but a fire lighting the night.

The two of them stepped into an open space in the forest. The rain had stopped, the clouds had parted, and the stars peeked through.

The trees were felled and the land had been leveled in the area. In the center of the clearing was a brightly burning crimson bonfire.

A human figure stood between them and the flames.

With the blaze against their back, all Ix could make out was a black silhouette.

And it was odd.

He could tell they were wearing a coat. Its hem was so long that it brushed the ground. That much was fine. The odd part was the head. They must have been wearing a hat, one with a wide brim and a pointed tip. That wasn't strange in itself, either, but the size was totally abnormal. The brim was so wide that the sides drooped down, and the tip was so long that it bent over halfway up. It just seemed like a waste of fabric. Maybe they were exercising their neck with the weight.

Ix and Camilla trekked across the short grass, and they could now see a house on the far side of the fire. It was a grand estate, not just a cabin. A large, one-floor edifice made of wood.

The figure must have heard their footsteps, because they turned to watch their approach.

It wasn't just the shadows that made her look dark but also her utterly black outfit. Her long, straight hair was black, as were her eyes. It was all so dark that it seemed light disappeared in the space where she stood. All Ix could make out was her floating white face. She was taller than Camilla but shorter than he was. Her age…was hard to guess. She looked about as old as he was, but…

"M-Miss Witch!" called Camilla, her voice filled with excitement. "It's been a long time! I'm sorry for dropping by all of a sudden, but we were wondering if you would have a mewmose antidote. Though it might be rude of me to ask…"

©Enji

"You seem well, Camilla," came a surprisingly young-sounding voice from her small mouth.

"Ah, y-yes. I'm good!"

"And you?" The black eyes turned to Ix.

"I'm fine, too."

"I was asking your name."

"...Ix."

"Hmm." The witch raised an eyebrow. Her shoulders shook, and a laugh came from her mouth. "I see, snow... How interesting."

"Anyway, the antidote—" started Ix.

"Half a day," she interjected.

"Huh?"

"As long as you take the antidote for mewmose within half a day, you'll be fine. No need to rush."

"...Do you have one?"

"The word *ix*, meaning *snow*, has its origins in the word *vigosh*." The witch ignored Ix's question and continued to lecture. "Do you get it? *Vigosh* in modern Central Standard means *vanish*. Quite the pun, eh?"

She was the only one who laughed, but she didn't seem to mind. For a while, the only sounds in the forest were the crackling of the fire and her chuckles.

Camilla apologetically said, "Um, we—"

"You must be hungry," she said.

"Huh? Uh, well..."

"Wait just a moment."

The witch turned back toward the flames. Looking in that direction, Ix saw several skewers of meat near it.

Ix wasn't particularly peckish. It wasn't long ago that they'd had all they could eat, and he was more worried about Yuui than anything else right now. This wasn't the time to be talking about hunger.

Focusing his nose on the scents in the air, Ix took in a whiff of burning wood mixed with roasted meat.

The witch eats people...

He remembered the tales, of course.

Thoughts ran through his head. *Could it possibly be...? But no...* He turned to Camilla, who stood beside him, but she seemed to be staring fervently at the witch. Her hands were clasped in front of her chest, and her eyes sparkled. Camilla admired her.

That continued for a short while until it seemed the meat had finished cooking.

"Now then," murmured the witch as she lifted the skewers. She wrapped cloth around the handle of the skewers and gave one to Ix and one to Camilla.

"Th-thank you!" said Camilla, but Ix frowned.

"...What is this?"

"I-Ix!" she chided in a low voice. "I know you're concerned about the rumors, but it's rude to—"

"That's not what I'm asking about."

Ix pointed at the skewer he'd been handed.

On it was a sad-looking, blackened lump.

The meat on Camilla's skewer and on the witch's looked exactly the same, though the witch had already pulled hers off and was chewing.

"Do you not like meat?" she inquired, her mouth moving up and down as she chewed.

And here Ix thought the thing had been so blackened that it was no longer edible.

8

As his eyes adjusted to the darkness, the light of the bonfire alone was enough for Ix to see the area around the house. Not that there was much besides it. This was just a simple clearing.

But when he went behind the house, he found something strange.

There were square white stones, set at equal intervals.

Four in the rear line and three in the front. They were neatly aligned in the two rows, with only one missing from the far right of the front line.

Upon closer inspection, they all looked quite old. The most ancient seemed to be the leftmost one in the back row. It was covered with moss and was almost entirely merged with the ground. The other stones were weatherworn and discolored, so it seemed as though quite some time had passed since they'd been placed there.

This was obviously not a naturally occurring phenomenon. A person must have arranged them.

"Aren't you cold?" came a voice from above. "Come inside."

He turned back and looked up to find the witch standing on the roof of the house. She leaped lightly and descended to the ground. It was such a graceful fall that her time in the air seemed to extend unnaturally.

"The antidote?" asked Ix.

"It's been mixed together. We just need to wait a little longer."

"Thank you."

"What's this? It's the least I could do for visitors; I don't get many."

"…These." He was lost for words for a moment. "Are they grave markers?"

"You're clever."

"Graves of the people you ate?"

"Yes." The witch nodded immediately.

"…Are you going to slurp someone down at this year's festival, too?"

"Hmm, I might not go to the festival anymore." She cocked her head. "I've been thinking it might be time for the witch to end."

"Huh?"

"Anyway, you should come inside. You'll freeze," she said, then trotted away.

When he entered her home, he froze in place as he stared at the wall.

"What is this...?" he muttered in amazement, but he of all people would already know the answer.

Wands and staffs.

A ton of them.

Short ones, long ones, hanging in huge quantities. There were far more than in the shops of his fellow apprentices. The terrifying thing was their range of ages. If his appraisal of them was correct, there were some from the dawn of the man-made wand revolution, as well as new styles that had been developed in the past few years. All these valuable instruments had just been casually thrown here. The sight of it all made him want to scream and scold her.

"Ah well, when you are what I am, you just sort of gather wands and staffs," explained the witch with a shake of her head. "Though, if you can use one wand, then they're all the same."

"In the corner there...that looks like an original Rednoff type."

"Yes, Rednoff brought it to me. A very unpleasant man, but his wands were a brilliant invention."

"......"

"Don't just stand there—come sit," said the witch to Ix, who was even more dumbfounded.

The room wasn't that large, but it seemed like a pleasant enough place to inhabit, complete with a small collection of daily necessities. There was a pair of couches facing each other, and Ix went to sit by Camilla, who was already on one. On the table in front of him sat a small vial. The cloudy solution inside was slowly settling.

"All right now." The witch sat across from them and crossed her legs. She still wore her hat inside. "Let's chat while we wait for the antidote to finish."

Ix stared at her face. It was so strange. That small, casual grin she wore looked so young, but she had an aura about her that went beyond age. That, and her dull eyes were the very embodiment of the word *inexplicable*.

"Your face says you'd like to ask me something, Ix," said the witch.

"…Where should I even start?" he said cautiously. "I've heard a few different rumors about you."

"Ask whatever you like."

"My master…Munzil. Did you know him?"

"Ah-ha-ha, that's what you want to ask first?" She brought her hand to her mouth. "Yes. I was acquainted with him."

Ix hesitated a moment, then said, "Are you a witch?"

"Yes."

"Are witches immortal?"

"Yes."

"Do you have more knowledge than humans do?"

"Yes."

"…Really?"

"Asking that would mean you have some way of proving otherwise, right? Since there's no point in confirming with someone you don't trust."

"No, sorry. I'll ask a different question." He knew what she'd said was right. "…Do you know Mali?"

"I haven't heard that name in so long." She smiled. "Mali… How many years ago was that? Have you met her?"

"Yes."

"What is she doing?"

"Not long ago, she was a head librarian."

"Aaah, books… Yes, how very like her."

"Do you remember anything about her?"

"Yes. When it comes to her and tomes… Oh, but are you actually interested?"

"No, I'm not." He wasn't particularly invested in her personally and knowing more about her wouldn't change anything. "But she's quit her job now and is bedbound in her mansion. It doesn't seem like she has much time left."

"...Oh. Has it already been that long?"

The witch touched the brim of her hat and adjusted it. The slight disturbance of air from that motion made the flames of the candles waver.

"Do you know that the capital's wand wall has been undone?" asked Ix.

"Has it really?" she asked with surprise in her voice.

"I don't actually know if it's true, but you're one of the suspects."

"Is that so? Well, I suppose I'll just deny involvement now, then."

Obviously, there was no point in Ix making further inquiries. He brought his fingers together and tented his hands.

"Just how long have you been alive...?" he asked after steeling himself.

"Well now... I'm not very good at counting the years. It's not like it's been one long line the whole time, either."

"How do you stay alive?"

"I eat people."

"...No, that's impossible," murmured Camilla.

"Camilla, I've told you so many times. You still don't believe me?"

"I just—"

"That...method," said Ix as he held up a hand. "How did you develop it? It's a technique far beyond what modern magicology can do. How could one person develop that on their own, and so many years ago?"

When asked, the witch suddenly smiled. She touched her fingertips to her lips and giggled. Her shoulders shook, like she couldn't stand how amusing it was. Ix was taken aback.

When her laughter eventually subsided, she gave a short answer.

"A dragon."

"...Huh?"

"Dragons. You know of them, don't you? They have infinite magic, expansive knowledge, and absurdly large bodies. Those ones. There were still many dragons living in the world when I was born. I met one of them and tried asking for something: its knowledge."

"That's ridiculous..." Ix pressed a hand over his mouth in shock.

"You don't believe me?"

"It's not that I don't think you're telling the truth..."

That answer would be somewhat against the rules.

If she said it was true, it didn't matter how big of a lie it was; Ix would have to take it at face value.

Dragons were unbelievably powerful, and they granted all wishes, without discrimination. If someone did come to possess their knowledge, they could actually become immortal.

But that was...

"It's just...," started Ix. "Even if you say it was a period of time when dragons still drew breath, if it was that easy to bump into one and receive their knowledge, wouldn't there be more people who would have it? More folks like you or others who inherited something else from them... And if that's true, then why would you be holed up in this forest? Despite the fact you have all this power..."

"Hmm, you seem to have come to the wrong conclusion..." The witch shrugged. "I was abandoned in the forest. Back during a period when these woods were even deeper."

""Huh?"" said both Ix and Camilla.

"My, was that a difficult time," continued the witch. "I'd never gone into the forest before that. I wandered about, eating nuts, berries, and grasses... By the time I realized it, I'd lost my way and had gone even farther into its depths. It's a miracle I wasn't attacked by magic beasts. But once, when I'd collapsed on the ground in exhaustion, the forest floor spoke to me. It said: '*I shall grant your wish.*'"

She closed her eyes as she remembered.

"I was thirsty and hungry, and more than anything, I wanted to go back home. I said, '*teach me what you know,*' and"—she spread her arms wide—"the witch was born. That's why I live here. All I wanted was the ability to save a small child—that's the only reason I have the dragons' knowledge. I have no intention of using it for anything more than that. That would be going against the agreement, wouldn't it?"

Ix felt sweat beading on his forehead.

She spoke as if it were fact, but it was all based on some assumption that went against common sense.

"Oh, that's right. You said something about the wand wall earlier," said the witch with a grin. "Can you fly?"

"Fly?" asked Ix.

"Can you fly using magic?"

"No…" Ix shook his head. "If that were possible…if that sort of spell were developed, then city walls would be meaningless."

"Exactly my point." She nodded. "If I left the forest, it would cause a huge fuss. It might be amusing, but I don't want to cause any trouble."

"Are you saying…y-you can? But using magic to fly is…"

"A form of magic humans will someday attain. Oh, but it's our secret for now. Everyone would be too surprised if they found out."

She's not human, Ix suddenly realized.

She was too far removed from being human.

This wasn't because she possessed knowledge and abilities that humans didn't. No, it was because her way of thinking lacked all humanity.

Dragons had still drawn breath roughly a thousand years ago. A human who had lived for that long…could no longer be called human at all.

There was no other word to call her by.

Hence, why she was now the witch…

Ix inhaled slowly and deeply.

"…Twenty years ago. You took a baby from the village," he said.

"Huh? Ix, where'd you hear about that?" asked Camilla in surprise.

"The villagers. And Gidens found a record of it."

"But you don't have anything to do with—"

"Now," said the witch as she raised a hand. "This is what he really wanted to ask. Go on."

"…Did you eat that baby?" he asked.

"No."

"Is that baby…me?"

The witch gave a knowing smile but didn't respond with either a yes or a no. Her black eyes bore into him.

"Tell me," he insisted.

"…Yes, it is," she revealed after a while, nodding.

Ix could hear Camilla gasp beside him.

The answer didn't shock him. He'd suspected as much based on what he'd researched so far.

"Why? Why did you take me, and why didn't you eat me? What happened twenty years ago?"

"Ix, you—"

Her voice didn't reach him. He shook his head; that wasn't it. That wasn't what he wanted to know. What he wanted to know was about what his own master had wanted from him…

"No, that's not what I want to ask. What I want to ask is why…?" He put his fingers together and closed his eyes. "Why am I alive? I was born from a mother with sonim. I am without magic. How do I still live? Is there…something else at work instead of that? Did I…get some power in exchange, like how you became the witch when you were abandoned? Is there anything like that?"

"There isn't," said the witch simply.

"…There isn't?" asked Ix, his voice rasping.

"No."

"Th-that can't be. If that's true, then how—?"

"Ix." She stood and looked out the window, her small back to him. "Sonim is just a disease. It was pure chance that you survived. When a mother has the infection, it stops the fetus's organs from developing. This isn't certain for every case, but multiple organs including the heart, brain, and lungs are destroyed as it progresses, hence why a scant few babies are born to infected mothers. But in your case, the symptoms only appeared in the organ responsible for mana. Yes, it was good fortune, pure and simple luck. You could even call it a miracle. But the fact that you're alive isn't a miracle. Besides, mana isn't necessary for living anyway. Horses and cows don't have any magical energy. It's the same as that. And so that's all it is. You were born without mana and were lucky enough to keep living like that… That's all."

"Then…," murmured Ix in his bewilderment. "What am I?"

"I knew that Munzil was searching for a human without mana," revealed the witch quietly. "I owed him, so I passed you to him. But even I, with all my knowledge of the dragons, am not privy to what the 'talent' is that he spoke of. That answers your question, does it not?"

There was an intermittent pattering sound.

The rain had started falling again. The intervals between each drop grew shorter and shorter.

Camilla, who had been listening to the conversation in silence, looked at Ix.

"Hey…Ix. Is that true? You were born here…?" she asked.

"Hmm? …Yeah, seems like it."

"Oh…" For some reason, her head was hung low.

In a complete contrast, the witch waved a hand and said in a cheery tone, "Well, it's a good thing you came to see me before I ended, Ix."

"I didn't exactly get much information, though," he replied.

"It's boring when you finally get the truth." She sighed.

"What?" Camilla raised her voice. "Wait, what do you mean by you ending?"

"Just that, Camilla," she replied. "I've been thinking it's about time for the witch to end. I don't eat people anymore, so I don't plan on going to the festival tomorrow."

"Wh-why?"

"Devouring people is a horrible thing to do, don't you think?" said the witch lightly. "I realized there wasn't much point in going that far. Besides, recently...there was someone who'd hung on for a thousand years but finally gave in. Maybe it's my time as well."

As she spoke, she turned her eyes to Ix.

That would mean...

She knew.

"Is there...anything I can do? Is there any way I can help...?" asked Camilla.

"Thank you, Camilla. But there's nothing that could help me."

"But..." Her shoulders slumped. "But if you're gone, what will happen to the festival?"

"The festival? Everyone is afraid of me and just runs. I imagine it will grow peaceful after this."

"Why do you also have to...?"

"Now, now, don't be so glum." The witch placed a hand on her shoulder. "Ah, good timing. Looks like it's done."

The white cloud inside the vial on the table had completely settled, so that the mixture was divided into the white precipitate and a pale-green liquid above it. The witch picked up another empty vial and poured the green liquid into it. She told them they should administer it in two doses, which would be plenty to counteract the poison.

It was pitch-black outside. The witch lent them a hooded lantern because it was dangerous in the dark. The lantern was small, but since there were no other lights around, it brightly illuminated the forest.

"And then… Ah, yes. We wouldn't want you to get lost. I'll give you a guide," said the witch.

"A guide?" asked Ix.

The witch gave a sharp whistle.

A moment later, they heard a low grunting approaching from the forest.

"Eek!" said Camilla, giving a small shriek of fright.

Her reaction was to be expected, because what came out of the forest was a magic beast.

Red in color, the creature was obviously a meat-eating type. It was an enedo.

Yet, while an enedo's most prominent feature was its curved teeth, this one didn't have any. They appeared to have been cut off at the base. It grunted at the same volume the whole time it slowly moved closer and closer to them.

"No need to be so frightened," said the witch as she held out a hand. The enedo, despite being a creature known for its violent tendencies, just sniffed at her hand. "Look, nothing scary here. He'll guide you to the edge of the forest."

"…I just remembered something I haven't asked," said Ix with a hand on his forehead. "Did you recently give a pair of adventurers a large amount of enedo teeth?"

"Hmm? Oh, you meant that." She nodded slightly. "I was in the forest, and they came to my house. They seemed to want them, so I let them take the teeth. These creatures here, their teeth make them a bit arrogant. They calm down quite a lot when you cut them off, as you can see. They stop fighting with other enedo, and they listen to what I tell them. They're very helpful for investigating the forest. Oh, but keep that a secret, too."

"Those two adventurers said you threatened them…"

"Threatened them? Why would I do something like that? I just gave them the teeth and said they should submit them to the Guild."

"…Why would you tell them that?"

"No real reason why…" She blinked in confusion. "I don't know much about it, but I thought that was what adventurers did?"

"…Okay. That's enough for me."

Apparently, the dragon's knowledge did not encompass common sense.

CHAPTER 4

The Witch Is Gone

1

Ix woke to the sound of excited voices. He looked outside to see large crowds milling about, enjoying themselves in the light drizzle.

When he left his bedroom, he found Yuui, Nova, and Camilla already eating breakfast. It looked like gruel.

"Good morning," said Yuui.

"How are you feeling?" he asked before anything else.

"Thankfully, I'm doing perfectly fine. There aren't any effects from the poison, right?"

"Yes," said Nova with a nod. "If no symptoms have developed by now, you should be, fine."

"That's good," said Ix.

"I heard you went out for my sake last night. Thank you," said Yuui.

"It's Camilla you should be thanking, not me."

"She's already done that." Camilla laughed. She held out a bowl of gruel to Ix, who accepted it with a "thank you."

"Where's Gidens?" he asked.

"He had to run off to the festival early in the morning," said Camilla. "It looks like none of the other food had mewmose on it. I've been racking my brain about it and wondering if it wasn't on the dishes instead…"

"Hmm…"

They didn't know if the poisoning had been accidental or deliberate. And regardless of intent, the question of where the mewmose came from still lingered. It seemed that this incident might just cloud their moods.

Camilla brought her hands together, as if to say there was something else to focus on.

"Today's the festival. You three should go have fun."

"Yes, thank you. And, um…," said Yuui, looking at Camilla hesitantly.

"Hmm? Oh, I'm fine. I'm not good with crowds. Don't worry about me."

"A-all right."

Camilla saw them off with a hearty wave, and the three of them decided to wander around the festival. The job for Layuma-tah and their investigations into the witch were over, letting them feel relaxed.

The majority of people from other villages had come early in the morning, and the tranquil sights from yesterday were like a different world compared to this, with people overflowing from the roads. In the end, it was almost like they'd brought Leirest here. The main part of the festival mostly occurred in the village square, but the road there was already filled with celebratory chaos.

The sight of small children dashing about in excitement was enough to bring smiles to their faces, but the young people were celebrating in a frightening manner. There were people dancing while cross-dressing, bounding into the fields, shouting absurd things, and propositioning literally anyone they laid their eyes on. They were the kinds of things that might make you question someone's sanity if they were happening on a normal day, but this was actually what the festival was all about…

As they strolled, Ix told Yuui about what happened the night before. They'd turn back every once in a while to make sure Nova was still there, a few paces behind them. He didn't know whether she could hear his report or not, but she wasn't showing any reaction to it.

"I see... So there was a misunderstanding between the adventurers and the witch...," noted Yuui.

"Yeah, seems to be something dumb like that. They'll probably be a bit relieved if you let them know."

"What do you think, Ix?"

"About what?"

"About the witch's story," she said, raising her head. "Just as Morna said before, we have no way of proving that the witch eats people, that she's immortal, or even that she possesses that knowledge. It all hits a wall when she says she got it from a dragon... But what was your impression? Can we trust her account?"

"Who's to say...? Not like I have the ability to see through lies." Ix shrugged. "But I do have thoughts on the wands."

"...That's very like you. Go on, then."

"If my eyes were right, I saw an original Rednoff-style wand hanging on the wall with the others."

"I believe I have heard of that in class...," said Yuui as she tilted her head. "It was the oldest type of man-made wand, yes?"

"It's the method that Rednoff used in the beginning; he's the one who developed the base theories of wands. That was two or three hundred years ago. There have been all sorts of advancements to create far more effective varieties since then, so those types of wands are no longer made. And no longer used. It's said there are only a few still in existence."

"Are you claiming this as supporting evidence for her story?"

"Is it not strong enough?"

"Well, does it mean that you believe her, Ix?"

"Hmm, well. I'm not sure I can really put it into words, but..." He hid his mouth with his hand. "For some reason, the way she talked just felt different. Honestly, it didn't seem like I was speaking with a living human. It was as though she were floating slightly above the ground... That's the sensation I got when talking to her."

"And have you moved on?" she asked suddenly.

"What are you talking about?"

"You asked about yourself, I assume."

"There wasn't really any closure...," said Ix, his expression unchanged. "I just confirmed what I already suspected was true. Besides, I wasn't particularly bothered by it in the first place."

"I see."

While they talked, they eventually reached the village square.

The adults seemed to have control over the situation here, as there was still a certain level of order, but the fervor of the large crowds was still overwhelming. Meat was being passed around everywhere, drinks were being poured for one and all, and red-faced townspeople let out boisterous guffaws.

They walked in the direction of a delicious smell that was drawing them in, which was where they found Gidens, busily grilling meat. There were several other villagers with him.

"Hmm? Ah, you lot," he said with a smile as he looked in their direction. "Ha-ha, too bad, though. If you'd come a bit earlier, you could've seen the cow get butchered. Now, we've only got meat left."

"That is perfectly fine for me," said Yuui with a sigh.

"Well, today's got nothing to do with who lives here or who doesn't. Eat up!" he said and handed over three skewers of meat. Nova took all three of them. This meat didn't appear to have any seasoning on it, but the people around them were biting into it with zeal.

They picked up a variety of other foods that were laid out and moved to the edge of the village square.

Perhaps Nova was somewhat hungry, because she bit into the food before anyone else. Ix tried taking a bite of the meat as well and found that it was incredibly tough. If he didn't chew it thoroughly, he'd risk it getting caught in his throat. It seemed eating the meat with zeal was actually a necessity. Still, this was a new experience for him, as he so rarely had the opportunity to indulge in beef, so he kept chewing away. The flavor was completely different from fish. He was mystified by the fact that something living on land could be this different-tasting from something that lived in water.

While Yuui was chowing down in enjoyment, Nova was beside her reaching for new food after new food. Her mouth never stopped moving.

After a moment of rest, Ix suddenly asked, "Yuui, can you fly?"

"Uh, what?" she asked back as she looked at him.

"It came up when I was talking with the witch. Whether or not someone could fly using magic. What do you think?"

"Magic-propelled flight… Yes, many theories have been put forward in the past for it, and it still comes up from time to time as a topic of debate… So, in simple terms, I would say yes, it is theoretically possible."

"Really?"

"Yes. Hmm, how should I explain it…?" Yuui set down the food she was holding and folded her arms. "For example, if one was to fire magic forward, the recoil would apply a force to the caster that pushes backward. The more powerful the magic, the more powerful the recoil. Which means, if one fired a spell at their feet, there would be a force propelling them upward. And truth be told, that does allow people to jump higher than normal."

She held up a finger and continued.

"However, just as I said earlier that it was *theoretically* possible, there are a number of already identified hurdles between leaping and flight. First, even if one were to reach the sky, it would take a huge amount of mana to maintain altitude. Next, 'flight' isn't simply getting into the air. You would still have to move forward, which would require constant expulsion of magic behind and below. On top of that, you would have to finely control that magic so as not to throw off your balance. I've read papers on the topic, but I honestly believe it would be impossible with current techniques."

"Uh-huh—" There were parts that Ix couldn't grasp because

he himself was incapable of using magic, but he understood the logic.

"Um, excuse me," interjected Nova after swallowing the food in her mouth. "Do you mean, current techniques within magicology?"

"...No, actually," said Yuui, looking down. She prefaced that this was just her own opinion before continuing. "I mean techniques using current wands. I believe you would need a specialized wand or staff for flying... Ah, I don't mean to say current models are bad, just that it's a mechanical matter."

Ix couldn't help furrowing his brows.

Was something like that possible?

Based on what Yuui had just said, you'd first have to branch the magic conduit partway down and create at least two outlets. Then you would need some mechanism to adjust the volume of mana being discharged in response to positioning. And if that couldn't maintain high transmission efficiency, the user would run out of magic energy. Actually, humans probably didn't have enough mana in the first place...

A cold sensation ran down his spine, making him shudder.

It was like stepping out into the dark, without any ground underfoot.

He couldn't think of a single solution for what he'd just been considering.

Could humans really achieve that someday? It was, at the very least, impossible for him.

"A wand like that...," he muttered.

"I-Ix, it's just a thought of mine. You don't have to think so seriously about it," said Yuui as she placed a hand on his back. "Would you like something to drink?"

"Yeah..."

He took a sip from the cup she handed him.

After a little while, a performance of musical instruments began in the center of the village square. A group of people sat on the ground in a circle, flutes and drums in hand. Their playing seemed free-form but surprisingly complex. Crowds gathered around them and clapped to the beat or added in whistles. Others danced in time.

"Mm." Nova suddenly looked up from her plate and cast her eyes left and right.

"What's wrong?" asked Yuui.

"I just felt, someone watching us."

"Huh…" Yuui tilted her head. "You can sense eyes on you? Is that specialized training as well?"

"It's, a figure of speech. What it really means, is that I saw someone looking this way, though it was from the corner of my eye, not in the center of my vision."

"Did you find them?" asked Ix.

"No." She shook her head. "They seem to have, hidden."

"Is this really something to be concerned about? We are unusual visitors here," said Yuui.

Sometimes, a villager would notice them standing by the edge of the gathering and come over to offer them alcoholic drinks. In the square, there was beer, fruit wine, and the oh-so-special mead. The same sweet scent from before spread to fill the area.

"No, I don't need any," said Ix, turning down the offer.

"Well, you're boring…," griped the man with a frown, a cup of alcohol in each hand. "How 'bout the two of you over there?"

Both Nova and Yuui shook their heads but didn't say anything. The man clucked his tongue in annoyance, then left.

"Ix, do you not drink?" asked Yuui.

"I don't understand why people have to do it. Actually, I want to ask them why they *want* to."

"Hmm, I don't really get it myself, either. It seems they have fun doing it, though…"

"Would've thought a festival would be enough. Not like the children are getting sloshed."

"Perhaps it's the opposite, and they're drowning their sorrows."

"Sorrows?"

"Yes. Alcohol is served at funerals and other such occasions in my country. I've heard it's for dulling painful emotions."

"If that's true, then why can't children drink it?"

"I don't know; I've never had any, either...," said Yuui as she looked at him. "But your saying all that must mean that you're having a good time, yes?"

"Huh? No, I—"

"...Hee-hee."

She chuckled as he fumbled for a reply. He couldn't see her face, since it was hidden beneath her hood, but her shoulders shook slightly.

After her bout of laughter, Yuui said, "Would you mind if I step away for a little while?"

"What's this about?" he asked.

"I just thought I would take some of this food over to Camilla."

"Oh..."

"Yes, go on," said Nova with a small nod. "I will wait, for you, here."

"Huh? Are you sure?" asked Yuui.

"Sure about, what?"

"Well, you're sort of my surveillance..."

"I don't think there will be any issues, if we separate slightly in this village."

"Oh..." Yuui tilted her head slightly, then looked at the food arranged in front of her. "Um, I'm sure this can't be the case, but is it that you would like to eat more?"

"No," said Nova immediately.

2

Nova watched Yuui as she picked up freshly cooked food from the square, then said, "Let's go."

"Huh? Where to?" asked Ix, but Nova was already a few steps away by the time he asked. She slipped deftly among the people gathered in the square. Ix managed to catch up with her.

While still facing forward, she said, "I was only able to do a broad inspection, but there was no mewmose."

"…You were eating to taste test for poison?"

"Yes." Her eyes showed as her bangs swayed. "The mewmose, was only on the food we ate. In other words, we can assume the mewmose was added, on purpose."

"Who did? Why? And who were they targeting? asked Ix, thinking on it as he did. "Gidens? He's the only one who could've put it on the meat."

"Yes, I thought so, too, at first. That he was the most, likely suspect."

"Which means it's not him? How do you know?"

"Now." She pointed ahead.

She gestured to a figure hiding in the shadows of a building, watching Yuui as she walked. They wore black vestments. It was Gidens.

"It's him, then, isn't it?" insisted Ix.

"No. If it were, he wouldn't hide like that; he would have just put it on the meat he gave us earlier. No matter who the target was, he could have poisoned them directly. And last night, he was also alone with Yuui, but didn't do anything to her. I believe he's doing that, because he's figured out who put the poison on the meat. He's not watching Yuui; he's keeping an eye out for the culprit."

"So then…she's the target? But why?"

Nova didn't answer. She approached Gidens from behind, walking so naturally, it almost looked like she was out for a stroll. She placed a hand on his shoulder, and he spun around violently.

"Hello," she said and bowed her head.

"A-ah, Miss Bangs… What are you doing here?"

"The same, as you."

"The same…?"

"Anyway."

Yuui had stopped walking and glanced to the side. She hadn't noticed them. Instead, she was looking at the storage building they'd carried the cargo into the day before, when they'd arrived in the village. It looked like someone inside had called to her. She gave a small nod and went into the building.

Gidens cursed under his breath and ran in that direction. Nova chased after him immediately.

She called to him. "We'll block the rear entrance."

"O-okay. Not sure how much you can do, but grateful for the help!" he replied.

"Yes."

Having been included in "*we*" all of a sudden by Nova, Ix did as he was told, though he wasn't entirely happy with the situation. This was the first he'd heard of a rear entrance to the storage building.

They pressed their ears to the back door once they got there.

"Hey, if you need help, I'll lend a hand," they could hear Gidens saying. "Can't go making our guests work for us; we get so few of them."

"Are you sure?" said Yuui.

"Yessir, miss. You get out of here."

"Thank you," she said; then they could hear light footsteps receding. Ix felt relieved.

Gidens's voice moved just a little closer. "What the hell's this all about? You saying you've got some grudge against visitors who just arrived in town yesterday? You could at least tell me why. We're friends, right? Just put down the ax—"

Having listened to that point, Nova quickly bent her legs and kicked in the door. The sound was hard on the ears but probably wouldn't stand out amid the hustle and bustle of the festival. Ix followed her into the building.

Gidens's face was just visible against the backdrop of the dimly lit storage building. A man with broad shoulders carrying an ax stood between Gidens and the trio. He turned his scowling face briefly to glance at them.

"Can we just have a calm chat, Gus?" proposed Gidens with his arms spread.

The other man, his chubby face red, tightened his grip on the ax.

Nova pulled a wand seemingly out of thin air and trained it on him.

Gus slowly turned to face her and said in a low voice, "…Visitors, I've been told about your strength. Particularly how you're good in a brawl."

Nova said nothing and didn't move an inch.

"But at this close a distance, and this difference in size, I've got the advantage," continued Gus. "Let me by."

"She's got a wand," pointed out Ix from behind Nova.

"I know. But I also know you chose to use martial arts in a situation when you could've just used magic. Which means…you can't actually use it, can you? No one would think of using a wand as a distraction."

"Huh, is that true?" asked Ix, unable to stop himself.

"Yes," replied Nova in a quiet voice.

"Ha-ha, I knew—"

Just as Gus went to raise his ax toward her, a purple beam shot from her wand.

There was a thud, and Gus sprawled out on the ground.

No one said anything for a while. It wasn't until after Nova had confiscated the ax and tied up Gus that Gidens let out a low "no way…"

Once the assailant regained consciousness, he looked like he'd aged significantly. There was no energy in his expression, and his personality seemed completely different from moments before.

"…I'm not going to try and make excuses for myself, like I was overcome by something," he said, his head hanging low.

"Hey, you can be all down on yourself, but unless you were

©Enji

possessed by an imra spirit back then, I want to know why you did that," demanded Gidens, crossing his arms. "I mean, you just met that young woman yesterday, yeah?"

"Yeah, but..." Gus's head hung down, and he spoke as if he had to squeeze every word out of his lungs. "That visitor's an easterner."

"Huh? ...Really?" Gidens looked over at Ix. "Actually, no, don't answer that. It'll cause all sorts of problems if it's true. But I get it now..." He closed his eyes and rubbed his chin. "You don't have to say nothing, Gus—she's the kind of person you've got a grudge against. Maybe it ain't even that, and you just wanted to take out your anger on someone."

"......"

"Could someone please, explain the situation?" asked Nova.

"Not even sure I'd call it a situation. It ain't that complicated," said Gidens with a wave of his hand. "Gus's son died in the Lukutta war. That's all."

After a long silence, Gus said, "It was the letters."

"Letters?"

"This one time, there was a letter mixed in with some goods that came up from Leirest. I thought it was a mistake, so I sent it back, but a reply came mixed in with the goods again. This time addressed to me. It said such dumb things, but my son had recently died... I just kind of kept writing responses. And the message that came yesterday said... It said there were three young people heading to Notswoll and that one of them was an easterner. Talked about the heroic stuff you did at the banquet in Leirest, too, little miss."

"The letter told you to kill Yuui?" murmured Ix.

"No, it didn't." Gus raised his head for a brief moment, then stared back at the floor. "...This isn't just some excuse I'm making now, but I didn't have any intention of doing her in. Not a single bit of me wanted to kill her when I first met her, either. I just wanted to talk a bit... That's what I was thinking when I called her into the storage building. But then the excitement of the festival got to me, and for some reason, I had this strange feeling come over me. By the time I realized it, I was standing there, holding the ax... No, that's probably just some excuse."

He let out a heavy sigh.

"I did something unforgivable," he continued. "I know I can't just apologize and have it forgotten. You visitors can decide what should happen to me."

Even with him saying that, Nova and Ix could only look at each other. It wasn't their right to decide his fate—it was Yuui's.

Gidens, who had been listening to the confession in silence until then, said, "Hey, you two. I know this is a lot to ask, but... could we keep what happened here a secret and let me deal with him?"

"Why...?" asked Gus, his eyes wide as he looked up.

"You know, I'm kind of supposed to serve the Lord," said Gidens. "Gus and I've known each other for a long time, so I believe I can get him back on the right track. Though, not much I can do if y'all don't have faith in me..."

Ix and Nova looked at each other, trying to decide what to do.

"To be honest, I don't really care," said Ix. "It's not like we'll be coming back here."

"I feel, the same," added Nova.

Gus closed his eyes in surprise and slowly lowered his head.

"Well, not sure how I feel 'bout the reason, but I appreciate it. Thanks," said Gidens, his expression more serious than they'd ever seen, though it was quickly replaced with a casual smile. "But you know, Gus. Maybe you put that poison on the meat knowing I would take it, or maybe you thought I wouldn't die, too. But if that little lady over there hadn't been with us, we'd all be in heaven now."

"Poison?" Gus blinked in confusion. "What poison?"

"What do you mean? The mewmose you put on the meat last night..."

"I—I don't know what you're on about. Like I told you, it was just a bit ago that I lost it. The ones who got your food together last night were those kids you asked for help…"

"…What?"

Nova dashed from the building like an arrow loosed from a bow. Ix hurried after her.

"It was a decoy," she said quickly. "There's another person who got a letter."

"Why is someone going to this much trouble to target Yuui?" asked Ix.

They arrived at the village square but couldn't find Yuui. She'd probably picked up a meal for Camilla and was already heading to her place. But if a villager had recommended some food to her during that time…

But they did have the antidote. If she happened to ingest a small amount of poison, it shouldn't be an issue. Ix couldn't bring himself to think about what would happen if she swallowed a large quantity.

For now, he and Nova just tried to cut through the crowds. Though they shouted for people to let them through, the festival goers didn't quite catch them between the excitement of the celebration. Quite the opposite—people started to think it was a new way to make noise, and soon the din grew even louder.

Despite that, they somehow managed to make it through the chaos. Just then, someone tugged on Nova's clothing.

"Hey," came a voice from below their eyeline.

"…Yonda?" murmured Ix.

It was the little girl who had spoken to Ix when they'd arrived in the village.

She held up a bowl toward Nova with both her hands. It contained a translucent liquid.

"Hey, lady, drink this," Yonda insisted.

Nova crouched down and took the bowl. She carefully tilted it and touched the liquid to her tongue.

With a slight tilt of her head, she murmured, "…I see."

"It's yummy, isn't it?" asked Yonda with a happy smile. "Will you show me your face now?"

"My, face?"

"Yeah. You're always hiding it. I want to see it."

"Before that, Yonda."

"What?"

"Do you, have a letter?"

"A letter?"

"With the powder, that you put in this."

"Yeah, I have it."

"Can, I see it?"

"Sure!"

She produced a small scrap of paper from her inner pocket.

"…I see," said Nova with a nod after she passed her eyes over the message. "Yuui never spoke in front of you, did she? So you assumed, she was a man."

Ix took the paper from Nova and read it for himself. The following was written in simple language:

There is a lady who always hides her face. Sneak this into her food. She'll be delighted.

3

They left Yonda in Gidens's care while the two of them went back to the rear entrance of the storage building. Thankfully, the door was of a simple make, so they were able to repair it with the tools that were already there. They opened and closed it several times to test it. It creaked a bit, but probably not enough that anyone would complain.

"All right, let's go back to the square," suggested Nova, but Ix called her to a halt.

"You really not going to tell Yuui?" he asked.

"Tell her, what?"

"That you're not surveilling her. That you're actually doing the opposite."

"What, do you mean?"

"You're good at lying." He sighed, then continued. "If Yuui trailing off and doing her own thing was a problem, you'd have no need to follow her around like this. They could just put her on house arrest in the capital. But you haven't been doing that, Nova. In fact, you let her do whatever she wants. You respect her ideas and actions. So then, who are you on guard for?" Ix stared out the storage building. "You're watching for anyone who might attack Yuui. That's it. What happened just then made that abundantly clear."

"......"

Nova froze for a while, seemingly considering something. Eventually, she pulled her chin in slightly.

"You are, correct."

"And you're fine not telling her? I'm sure Yuui would feel relieved that you're her guard, not her surveillance."

"You misunderstand." Her bangs swayed. "I am her guard, but I am not her ally. I am protecting her, so that we can use her. Telling her that, would be even worse."

"Use her? But she—"

"Has no value as a hostage, beyond appearances. We already know that. She has been abandoned, both by the kingdom, and by Lukutta. That was, until not long ago."

"What happened then?"

"The Academy exam."

"Huh?"

"In the exam, she placed fourth in her class. She has far surpassed most typical students, in both normal studies, and in magic usage."

"That's...incredible." There was nothing else Ix could say to that.

"More abnormal, than incredible." Nova nodded. "There was apparently, no formal education system in Lukutta. Yuui started learning, both academically and magically, when she came to the Academy. In the beginning, she didn't even know the language. But in one short year, she took fourth place. The kingdom is embarrassed, to put it bluntly. Publicly, they announced she placed forty-eighth."

"…Won't she notice something fishy with that? A discrepancy between how the test seemed and how the results came out?"

"She has too low, an opinion of herself. She seems to believe most of her ability, comes from the wand. In light of that, she will assume that when evaluating the exam, they took her wand into consideration, and evaluated her on skill alone."

"A wand's duty is to let a magic user use their power to its fullest potential. No matter how amazing it is, it can't make someone more capable than they naturally are."

"She once told me it was just because her wand was special. I don't understand what that means. Do you know anything about that?"

"…No," deflected Ix with a silent shrug.

"Anyway, that's what led to some viewing her as a danger. If she were driven to the edge at the Academy, many students could wind up dead."

"That would never happen."

"I, concur," said Nova. Ix sensed there was a misunderstanding but didn't say anything. "On the other hand, there are powers at play who have come to see her ability, as something they can take advantage of. Those people dispatched me."

"I'd like to know who those people are."

"The Reformation Sect."

"…So you're New Order, too?"

"Yes. We have infiltrated the Church, and are waiting for our opportunity, to instigate a revolution from within. In that regard, the Secession Sect's actions have been too reckless. If they carelessly incite a revolt, it will hinder our own plans. That's why, the incident at the Obryles' mansion was so unexpected, and why we were lucky to resolve it so quickly. Thank you for your help, back then."

"So…," he said as he opened a hand, "how do you plan to use her?"

"No matter how peaceful a revolution we achieve, the kingdom will still be thrown into disarray. The impact of that will likely extend, beyond the kingdom's borders. We wouldn't want there, to be riots in the regions the kingdom controls. In order to prevent that, we will set in place leaders in those regions who are under our influence, and use them to control what transpires. We have already taken on board, a portion of those in positions of authority in Lukutta."

"You're…going to force Yuui into a leadership position in Lukutta? Are you serious?"

"Yes," she confirmed immediately, nodding. "Yuui will return home, and there she will have plenty of influence to achieve our ends, even without the kingdom's support, as long as she tries for it. That's how skilled a person she is. I evaluated the situation in that manner, and the higher-ups agreed with me, once I reported about the incident at the Obryle mansion."

"Wait, did you accept the job from Layumatah in anticipation of this happening?"

"No, I didn't." Nova looked down slightly. "But it has been, far too convenient. I feel like there was something at work, when Layumatah chose Yuui to help with this job. I think there may have been, a deal struck somewhere."

"Somewhere? Where?"

"Above." She pointed up, and Ix's eyes followed in that direction. She obviously didn't mean in that way, though.

"…Should you really be telling me this?" he asked.

"Yuui will figure it out eventually, sooner or later. But even if she does realize it, she'll act without regard to her own emotions, so long as she believes it's for others. That's the sort of person, she is. Once she considers, how many casualties there'll be if a chaotic rebellion breaks out in Lukutta, it'll be obvious to her that someone should rein it in. No matter how horrible a fate that person suffers, if they compare the numbers..."

"That's selfish of you."

"Yes. I'm stealing her life from her. It's, cruel."

The topic of conversation was far too massive for Ix to comprehend. It seemed like the world they lived in was different, or the scale they thought on was different. All he worried about was crafting wands or not; he couldn't fathom the burdens Yuui had to bear.

Nova spoke again.

"I don't know if they discovered, what happened at the Obryle mansion from other attackers who stayed hidden or simply through hearsay, but it seems some in the Secession Sect did find out. I believe the fact that she took control of the situation at the mansion, in conjunction with the opinions of those who view her as a threat, and those who have certain feelings toward easterners, is somehow connected to the orders given to the villagers."

After the attack at the mansion, Nova and the others had been questioned. Even if you didn't go out of your way to gather information, the banquet had so many influential people that information leaks were bound to occur.

"Their grooming of Gus and Yonda, was likely part of their original plan, their hopes to create a revolt during the festival to take advantage of. It seems they were set up rather quickly, though... Anyway, we can't leave people like that, to their own devices. I must return as quickly as possible, submit a report, and find them."

"Grooming..." Ix suddenly had the thought that he'd heard a conversation before about letters mixed in with goods, which was when he let out a gasp.

"What, is it?" asked Nova as she looked at him.

"It's just…uh." Ix tilted his head and blinked. He felt the energy leak from him, or at least the excitement. "The guard at the gate. It was him."

"What?"

"Well, I mean, it's not like anyone had any way of knowing we were even going to Notswoll. We decided to go in the middle of the night before. The only person we told was Morna. Unless someone saw Yuui on the streets that morning, they couldn't have written any letters."

"There were some travelers on the street. Some people would have been able to know, even if they weren't the guard."

"That's right. But there was only one person who could have put the letters in place, only one person who touched the goods. The guard who inspected the cargo when we passed through the gate. Which means… Oh, that's right." Ix covered his mouth with his hand. "The secret letter that said the wand wall had been undone was the same. It was just a ploy from the guard who found it or the soldiers on guard duty. That's how they had the correct security details to put in the letter."

"Some sort of, diversion?"

"Probably. Like…if someone was planning to incite a rebellion in Leirest, they might try to divert attention to the capital, right? Or anything, really."

"Should you not, contact Layumatah?" asked Nova pointedly.

"Well…" He frowned. "I figured it out, so she's probably realized it by now as well. I bet they've already arrested the guard or are keeping tabs on him."

Yeah…thinking about it now, it was obvious.

Undoing the wand wall was supposedly an impossible task in the first place.

Was this something unique to humans? Or was it just his own foolishness?

If something sounded like it could be true, Ix would carefully consider it, one step at a time. But if it was something questionable, he would accept it all at once and forget it was an assumption in the first place.

He'd been misled by the smoke screen of impossibility.

He'd been trapped inside.

Ah… Which means, the witch…

He felt as if his vision had cleared. The interconnected puzzle pieces started to fall into place, one after another. He likened the sensation to that child's game where you lined up small pieces of wood and watched them knock one another down in a line.

So that was the case. The witch was cruel.

Ix let out a heavy sigh.

It was good he'd considered this more.

It was good he hadn't just believed everything because she was a magical witch with the knowledge of a dragon.

And it was ever so apparent to anyone, so long as they thought about it…

"Yuui should be coming back, soon," said Nova to him. "Let's return to the square."

"No, I've got something to take care of at Camilla's, too. I'll pass her on the way there," he said.

"Oh, right."

They moved from the storage building into the square and returned to where they'd been standing earlier. It seemed the people had finally started to tire of celebrating. The instruments had stopped playing, and the villagers were relaxing. Ix looked down the road to see a figure in a gray coat approaching them.

"By the way…," said Ix, "I would've thought it'd be easier to protect Yuui if you kept her in one place—what's with letting her wander around like this? You trying to make up for what you're doing?"

"…Yes." Nova nodded slightly.

"Is that an order from above, too?"

"It's, my own decision."

"Why would you—?"

"Because, she saved me," replied Nova curtly. "At the time, we were just classmates. Even so, she helped me, the citizen of an enemy nation, solely because I needed help. I didn't understand why, but I've come to accept it as I've spent time with her. She is honestly, just an abnormally, good person." Her bangs swayed as she looked down. "If I can, I want Yuui to live as she dreams, in a peaceful place, with nothing connecting her to what's going on in the kingdom. That is my personal, wish. I let her do as she pleases, just to fulfill my own selfish desires."

After hearing that, all Ix could say was, "…Yeah," and nod.

Nova was completely correct.

Yuui had lost her family.

She'd been taken from her homeland.

She was alone in a foreign country…

Why? Why did someone who'd experienced such difficulties have to be subjected to even more? She defeats people from the Secession Sect; then people try to kill her; then she becomes the Reformation Sect's pawn.

But if Yuui thought that was the just thing to do, she would do it. She would search for a better way forward, worry about whether or not there was another option, help the people of her enemy country, and suffer endless hardships and heartache.

That had nothing to do with the wand or her father.

It was just her own honest goodness.

Even if she would be better off not getting embroiled in the kingdom's political wars, lost festivals, the legend of the witch, and all that…

If she wanted happiness for herself…

Ix took a few steps ahead, then suddenly turned back and said, "…I was thinking."

"There's, something else?" asked Nova as she looked at him.

"Even if you were taste testing for poison, you didn't really need to eat all that food, did you?"

"You, think so?"

4

Camilla was sleeping at the table.

She was lying sideways, her head on an outstretched arm.

She quickly noticed the other person across from her.

After sitting up, she looked at their face.

"...Yuui," she said.

"I thought you might be hungry," said Yuui as she placed food on the table. The pleasant aroma of food she couldn't normally enjoy wafted to her nose.

"Thank you. It looks delicious."

Camilla smiled, but she wasn't hungry, so she put the dish of food back after only a bite. Yuui didn't say anything as she watched. Rather than leave the house, she just gazed vaguely out the window.

Was she really here?

"Hey...," murmured Camilla, almost to herself. "Why does the witch have to disappear?"

There was no reply.

The rain outside was growing steadily stronger.

Camilla realized Yuui was staring at her.

"...Camilla," she said.

"Yes?"

"I've been thinking for a while now...," started Yuui thoughtfully. "It was a simple question I had in the beginning. The legend says the witch appears on the day of the Feast of Meat and devours a child. But if that was the case, the solution would be simple. Stop holding the festival." She looked down at her hands. "I haven't met the witch myself, and I don't know what she really is. And so I can't ask why she only appears on the day of the festival. But no matter how grateful the people are to their god, I cannot think of a reason why they would continue holding a celebration that would put them in danger. The only explanation that makes sense is that the villagers have something to gain from it."

"Something to gain? From children getting eaten?"

"It is an opportunity to eliminate someone without feeling guilty," continued Yuui emotionlessly. "Sometimes, a child can be a burden on an impoverished family. But they're also the easiest burden to discard. The parents can just make another one, after all. But the mental stress of doing something like that is far worse than, say, when you abandon an elderly person. So people might appreciate something that could do the deed for them."

"…That's what you think?" asked Camilla, and Yuui shrugged.

"It's only a guess. I have no way of confirming it. That was not what I've been thinking about; I've been thinking about what the witch's curse is. Have you heard of it? They say you have been cursed by the witch, which is why you've lost your family and your fortune."

Camilla's only response was slightly tucking in her chin.

"It is true that you've lost your parents and that your wealth was stolen. You live alone in this home with nothing in it, and it seems you don't use the well in town, so you have to travel far out to get your water. It's no wonder people say you're cursed."

"The witch would never hex anyone…"

"You're right—there is no witch's curse." Camilla felt as though Yuui's gaze was boring into her. "Throwing away your belongings, going outside the village for your water, those are things that *you* do. There is no external influence. Which means…there must have been something that led you to feel you had to curse yourself. Since you're such a good person, that was the only option."

"I'm…not a good person."

"No, you are. You simply want the people around you to be happy. I could never compete with someone as good as you."

"……"

"Let's go back to the witch. About twenty years ago, an ailing, pregnant woman came to this village. She gave birth around this time of year and died in the process. When the town held the Feast of Meat, the witch kidnapped the baby. However…" Yuui tilted her head. "Why did she abduct him? Sonim was rampant in the area at the time, and I've heard that the festival was nothing more than a small formal ceremony. So then why would someone bring a newborn along to it if they weren't the mother? Why would they drag the baby out of the house to a festival that wasn't that much of a fuss? And that's where the infant happened to be targeted by the witch... It's too unnatural a situation."

Yuui had probably figured out everything.

Her voice contained not a hint of blame or kindness.

"You just wanted to help someone, didn't you, Camilla?" asked Yuui.

"...Did Gidens tell you that?"

Yuui nodded.

"I see."

She just wanted...

She just wanted to help someone.

To help everyone.

That was all.

And though that was all she wanted...

Why did that have to happen?

Had she really thought it was a good idea?

She didn't know.

The sickness had been everywhere in the village, and everyone was suffering.

The baby was alone, his mother had died, and he was crying.

She was just asked to watch him for a bit, and he lay there in her arms...screaming.

No one in town had the ability to care for him right now.

How painful would it be for him to get hungrier and hungrier until he died?

That must have been why he screamed so much.

And so...

She pressed a flower into his little hand.

She hugged him.

She thought she would be thanked.

Because she'd heard that *she* ate things like this.

Surely, she would gladly accept.

She might even tell Camilla how she could become a witch.

That's what she'd thought…

"Will you tell Ix…?" asked Camilla as Yuui stood and placed a hand on the door.

"I had planned to at first." Yuui turned back to Camilla and smiled. "But I won't. It won't solve anything. It will only increase the number of people suffering."

"I see…"

"Do you want me to tell him?"

"No, don't."

"That's what I thought."

Without saying anything more, Yuui left.

She left Camilla alone in the room, alone with her selfishness.

Sometimes, she wondered why she was alive.

Why was she still alive when she hadn't even been able to save her sister?

Why was she still alive when her mom and dad had perished?

When they died, she'd felt like she was finally paying for her deeds…

But how could the villagers let her remain in the village, even though they knew what she'd done?

Vague thoughts passed through her mind, and she drifted off to sleep again.

When next she opened her eyes, a man stood in front of her.

"Ix?" she asked.

Was this a dream?

He sat across from her and put his elbows on the table. He seemed to be finding it difficult to say something.

"What's wrong?" she asked.

"I…" He placed a hand over his mouth. "I don't really understand. What's good for people? What's bad for people? I feel like it'll make things worse, and I feel like it'll make things better than they are. Personally, I think it's good, but maybe that's just my personal prejudices getting in the way... Which is why I want to leave it to you to decide. I doubt you'll be opposed to it, if you happen to want it as well. And I mean, she's just given up on it. And there are probably people who think that's for the better..."

"W-wait a minute," said Camilla with a confused smile. "I have no idea what you're talking about when you put it like that. I understand you're having a hard time, but could you explain from the beginning?"

"A-ah, from the beginning... Right, so it's like this..."

As she listened to the inarticulate man say his piece, she smiled. Why?

She was in this empty room...

Why was she so relieved?

5

The rain fell even harder once noon passed, but the bustle of the festival only grew, as if in protest. While the people clamored, they gathered to the already harvested fields. The adults lined the edges of the pasture, instruments in hand. The children and young people leaped into the fields with whoops and cries. The music eventually started, as did the dance, which concluded the Feast of Meat.

"Shall we...go back?" Yuui asked Nova as she gazed at the celebrating people.

"Yes," said Nova with a nod. "I had completely forgotten, there is a deadline we need to report by. I want to leave this village, as soon as possible."

"Night will fall while we're traveling..."

"We can camp near the city, so we'll be the first ones let in the next morning. We don't need to worry about magic beasts, so long as we get to the highway by the time night falls."

"If we do that, even though you're watching me, I can—"

"I would appreciate it if we traveled, together," said Nova as she stared at Yuui. "What do you think?"

"…Okay." Yuui sighed.

"Thank you."

"Not that I have any right to choose."

"Shall we, then?" Nova moved away from the fields as if to say they should leave as soon as possible.

As they did, they saw someone they knew coming quickly toward them.

"Is it over?" asked Ix as he looked at the fields.

"Well, I wouldn't really know if it's over or not," said Yuui with a quick glance at the fields. "Who knows when they'll stop dancing if the witch doesn't come. I feel like they are very much losing their enthusiasm…"

"Losing their enthusiasm?"

Yuui decided to tell him what she thought. "I have sort of been thinking that the witch's arrival has become a part of the festival. Just as Gidens said, she shows up, and everyone runs. That's what marks the end of the Feast of Meat, yes? They might be frightened of the witch, but I think they also need her."

"Uh-huh…"

Although that, too, was just a guess. There was a limit to what people could understand. As the two of them chatted, Nova cut in.

"Excuse me, Ix. We are heading back to Leirest, now. We must submit, our report."

"Report? Oh…yeah."

"Yes."

"What are you going to do, Ix?" asked Yuui.

"I don't have anything I need to do right away. I'm going back tomorrow."

"Then we will see you again in Leirest. Will you report to Layumatah in person?"

"No… I think a letter should be enough."

"Oh, okay."

She had been thinking that if he went to the capital, she would show him around a little, but there was nothing she could do about him not coming.

With that, Yuui bowed her head, but Ix stopped them.

"Before you go…can you help me with something?" he asked.

"What is it?"

"Call the witch."

"What?"

"Like you said before, it'll be bad if the festival doesn't end, see."

"I did say that, yes, but…how?"

The witch had supposedly said she wouldn't come to the festival anymore. By "*call the witch*," did he mean he was planning on going into the forest, knocking on her door, and asking her to make an appearance? Not that this bothered Yuui, but it was all a bit sudden.

Ix brought a hand to his mouth and looked up.

"Um… Oh yeah, that's it. Can you make lightning?"

"Lightning?"

"At the festival eighty years ago, they said the witch appeared along with a storm."

"She'll come if I make lightning?" Yuui cocked her head, wondering what he was saying. "And besides, I can't use magic to do that. There are only rain clouds here, not thunder clouds."

"You just need to make it seem like there's lightning. Put on a show, I mean."

"Huh…?"

Yuui wasn't entirely satisfied with his explanation, but she had to leave the village soon for Nova's sake. She thought she could make it at least look like there was lightning. It was basically just a flash and a bang. It would suffice if she shot out a brief white light, then produced a sound that resembled thunder. She wasn't particularly good at sound spells, though... She would just have to rely on the wand's power.

"I just have to make it look like it's lightning, right?" she asked.

"Yeah, if you don't mind," he replied.

She pulled her wand from her inside pocket. The villagers were focused on the fields, so they probably wouldn't notice.

Light and sound could cause damage if she went overboard. She closed her eyes and calculated how to adjust the power of her incantation.

Luckily, the rain was falling more heavily. When the music reached a particularly strong crescendo, she pointed her wand ahead.

She held her breath for a moment and created an intense light.

Her vision was blotted out with white.

She might have slightly overdone it.

Without a moment's hesitation, she loosed the sound, a roar like thunder tearing through the sky.

Yuui felt like it had sounded decent enough.

With that, she should have created an illusion of lightning striking behind the villagers. She quickly put her wand away.

In her mind, she'd done a pretty good job. And though she was relieved it had gone well, for some reason, no one turned around.

For a moment, she worried that the light had been too strong and temporarily blinded her, but that wasn't the case. In fact, while her vision was slightly hazy, the people weren't looking in her direction; there was something else on the other side of the fields that was far more deserving of their attention.

From the dim depths of the forest emerged a figure wearing a pointed hat and a black coat.

"The witch," said someone.

"The witch, the witch is here, the witch has come." Cries escaped people's mouths as they dashed away. Some joined hands with their family; some tugged the arms of someone of another gender, but all rushed to the village. Their faces looked the same: filled with terror and, oddly...perhaps a bit of amusement.

It would be strange to remain there, so the three ran alongside them. They felt no threat, though, so it was a jog at best.

As they ran, Yuui whispered to Ix, "That witch...looked like Camilla."

"Indeed," he replied with a matter-of-fact nod.

"What's this about?"

"I suggested to Camilla that if the witch wasn't coming to the festival, then she should dress up as one and come down herself. None of the villagers has ever seen the witch up close, so they wouldn't notice as long as she was dressed the same."

"Is there a point to doing that?"

"Nope, not at all."

Yuui stared into Ix's eyes. "Are you hiding something?"

"What would I be hiding?"

"...I'd just like to confirm, but you really did meet the witch in the forest, yes?"

"The witch?" replied Ix expressionlessly. "Nope, she was gone."

6

The rain lifted the next morning. Clouds still filled the sky, but few contained rain.

The remnants of the festival lay scattered in the streets and village square. The adults who had celebrated in a more responsible manner last night were cleaning them up. For most of the attendees, however, the festival was still continuing in their dreams.

Ix, with his things on his back, turned toward the direction of Leirest. A chilly wind swept across the empty fields. It was a gentle current, one that pushed the seasons to change.

People's memories of this festival would consist of eating all the meat they could want, drinking to their hearts' content, and having a huge celebration. Those memories, along with the hope of a spring soon to come, were the only things they had to get through the winter.

"H-hey!" someone called out.

He heard footsteps rushing toward him, so Ix turned around.

There stood Gidens, struggling for breath. He pressed a hand to his side—apparently he'd been in a rush to get here.

"Wh-what the hell's this about?" he asked, showing Ix a leaflet in his right hand. "Was this your suggestion, Ix?"

Ix leaned in to read the piece of paper. It was a letter from Camilla, addressed to Gidens, which read, "I've found a way to get a staff. I'm leaving for a little while to go learn magic. Thank you for everything."

"No, it's got nothing to do with me," deflected Ix with a shake of his head.

"H-how could it have nothing to do with you? You're—"

"She told me that she's been slowly saving up money, and she finally got enough to buy one. She figured no one would notice if she slipped out the day of the festival."

"Did she go to the capital? Or somewhere else?"

"Dunno. I didn't ask."

"……"

Gidens bit his lip but remained silent.

He stared at Ix for a while before finally muttering, "She hasn't run off to get married, has she?"

"Huh?"

"I-it's a joke," he said with his usual casual smile. "It's a joke, yeah, just a joke... Yeah, that's right; that's all it is..."

"She asked me to tell you thanks if I ran into you," said Ix.

"Ha-ha, well, that's an appropriate level of politeness coming from someone you've been close to for the past fifteen years. So polite, I might just cry." He shrugged; then his expression quickly grew serious. "Well then, just in case, if you ever happen to run into Camilla, I want you to tell her something."

"Tell her what?"

"Don't come back." Gidens let out a sigh. "Her happiness ain't in this village. It's been that way for decades. And it'll probably be the same in the future. I thought I could save her, but that didn't happen, either. So then, if, if she happens to find a happier place for herself, she should stay there. But we're talking about Camilla here. She's got some weird feelings about her birthplace, and I bet she'd try and come back. So just tell her for me—tell her not to do it."

"All right."

"…Actually, no, don't. Don't say that to her."

"You sure?"

"I don't want to give you a chance to look too cool," said Gidens with a sarcastic grin. But the next moment, he looked relieved. He raised his right hand and said, "See ya then, craftsman."

"I'm an apprentice."

"You seriously correct people every single time? That's got to be a pain; just hurry up and get certified already."

After saying his good-byes, Ix walked down the road. The houses came to an end, and the fields expanded to fill the entire landscape. There wasn't a single boundary line to mark the end of the village, but he thought he would be leaving Notswoll soon.

Suddenly, he stopped.

In a field off from the road was a square white stone. It was half buried in tall grasses. The one they'd seen on the way in.

At the time, he thought it might have been a border marker for the village or some sort of magic beast deterrent, but now he knew that wasn't the case.

He pushed the grass aside and walked up to stand in front of the object.

It was a gravestone.

He knew it wasn't a grave for a villager from Notswoll because it was the only one here.

As he stared at it, he heard the creaking of wheels turning in the distance.

With slow movements, someone came to stop immediately behind Ix. Without a word, they held a cup out to him.

Inside sloshed a golden liquid.

A sweet scent rose from it.

"You knew, didn't you?" asked Ix.

A pregnant woman, suffering from sonim and chased from her own hometown, had collapsed near the village, where someone found her. Though there were some who opposed bringing her back into the village, the person who found her insisted that they would care for her themselves.

A farmer, who had carried goods back and forth from Leirest, for the longest of times. Unlike the other villagers, who had no reason to leave town, he often passed along this road.

And it was he who had set up this gravestone...

The white-haired farmer said nothing.

He just held out the cup to Ix.

Ix accepted.

Just bringing the cup to his face was enough for the dizzying scent of the alcohol to hit him.

Holding his breath, he quickly poured some into his mouth.

A surprisingly gentle sweetness passed over his tongue.

"It's good," he couldn't help himself from murmuring.

"It's mead."

Ix started to remind the farmer he'd said that before, but then he stopped. Instead, he took another sip.

7

Yuui visited the shop again a few weeks after Ix had returned to Leirest. Nova tagged along as well, but she stood on the street without coming close.

Even though Ix was surprised, he invited Yuui into the shop, but she held up a hand in refusal. She looked around to check no one was there, then half lowered her hood.

"I'm sorry, but we have to leave very soon. I only came to say my good-byes," she explained.

"Good-byes?"

She placed her hands on top of each other in front of her. "I'm going back to Lukutta this time."

"Huh?"

"The shop is near a road in that direction, so I insisted we stop by."

Ix blinked a few times.

"Oh…," he finally managed to say. "That's…good."

"Yes."

"Do you know what you'll be doing there?"

"No… But I am the only one who has spent this long in the kingdom. I have been thinking that I might be able to contribute somehow because of that. I wonder if I might be able to do something for the people, even if it is not much."

"Oh yeah? Um…"

"It appears that a number of the guests at the banquet spoke on my behalf, insisting that I saved their lives."

"Uh-huh." Ix brought a hand to his mouth and looked at Nova standing at a distance. She responded with a slight nod.

"Well, I will obviously only be in Lukutta temporarily," said Yuui.

"When are you coming back to the kingdom?"

"The current plan is to spend about a year there, then come back next spring. Though the timing hasn't been set in stone, either, so it might be longer before I come back, and I most likely won't return to the Academy when I do. So many things are still undecided…" Yuui peered into the shop. "Um, are Morna and Ottou not in?"

"Ah, Morna's still sleeping, and today Ottou's not around… Should I wake her up for you?"

"No, that's all right. It's a little unfortunate, but please give them my regards."

"Sure thing."

"Ix…" Yuui's eyes wandered for a moment. "Are you making wands?"

"…You heard from Layumatah?"

"I did."

"I am, yeah. As much as I can anyway."

"What started it?"

"…It was that place," he said, tripping over his own words before holding up what he had in his right hand. "And this."

"It just looks like a stick," she said, a crease in her brow.

"Yeah, looked like just a stick to me, too. Do you remember? At the Obryle mansion, the man giving the speech had a fake wand. I tried asking if I could examine it, and he let me."

"You went out of your way to examine a fake wand?"

"I think it was probably the real deal." He waved the instrument. "I kept coming back to this over and over, but it really looked to me like it shot off a spell. If a weak, shoddily crafted stick like this can cast incantations, too, then it opens up a lot of possibilities. We could make wands smaller, or… Anyway, I'm doing research on that in addition to crafting."

"Hmm…" She tilted her head as she looked at him. "What benefit would there be for making them smaller?"

"Hmm…no clue. I'm just exploring a possibility."

"I see. I suppose that's just what a craftsman does."

"Maybe," he said, unsure.

Yuui slid her hand into her pocket and produced a letter. "Layumatah gave me this to bring."

"For me?"

"It's a response to the report on the job we did."

"Huh…"

That was a rare thing for Layumatah to send. When he took the envelope, it felt like there was only a slip of paper inside.

"Ummm..." Yuui looked at him. "There was something you said about the witch when we left Notswoll."

"What about it?"

"Was it true? That the witch was really just a woman living deep in the forest who was knowledgeable about herbs...?"

"Yeah," said Ix with a nod. "In truth, the word doesn't refer to a specific person. It's probably a general term that applies to any of the magic users in the group who lived in the forest. There's no point in having such a huge clearing for one house, which explains why she had wands and staffs from so long ago. And the reason they were able to use the emission method thirty years prior to everyone else was, well, I guess that's because they were just that powerful... But anyway, their band seems to have come to an end, too. In reality, the one witch I met didn't use any magic. That was probably the reason she said she was ending the witch. She wasn't making it end; it had to."

"But if that was the case...why were the villagers that frightened of her? I know magic users are uncommon, but if they knew the truth..."

"It's simple. It's better for them that way."

"What does that mean?"

"It's for the safety of the forest." Ix shrugged. "It's a miracle a forest like that still exists this close to a city. There would definitely be people who want to take the land. But before people like that snatch it up, they think, *Why are these woods still here?* They might think magic beasts live there or something. They don't want to find that out after they take the land. So they go to the village to check it out, and what happens? All the townspeople go on and on about this terrifying thing living in the forest. The fact that the forest still exists is actually proof of their claims. In the end, no one wants to touch a creepy place like that. It probably makes life easier for the villagers to have the resources of the forest at their doorstep."

"And that's...the witch?"

"It's just a theory. Can't really go and ask." Ix spread his hands. "They've been at it so long that the villagers might actually have come to believe it themselves... Doesn't really matter, though. At the very least, Mali truly believed it."

"You are denying that she eats people and is immortal as well, yes?"

"Yeah. The immortality is just your run-of-the-mill rumor."

"But—"

"Nova told you about the immortal creatures before, right?"

"Ah, yes," said Yuui, looking doubtful. "A portion of your own body is rejuvenated and released from you, whereupon it gains new life, and the process is repeated. If you define life in that way, you could argue that every living creature is immortal. It sounds like nothing more than a play on words to me..."

"That's all it is. There's no creature that lives for eternity."

Still looking unconvinced, from the side of the road, Nova called out, "Yuui."

"Oh..." Yuui looked back briefly, then turned to face Ix again. "I'm sorry, but I have to go. I need to return before snow falls."

"Right... See you then."

"Yes, good-bye."

She lowered her head and turned to walk away, but Ix called out to her without thinking.

"Wait, uh..."

"What is it?" she asked in confusion as she turned back.

"Can I call you Laika?" he asked, hiding his mouth with his hand and trying to sound like he normally did.

"Huh?"

"Well... I heard that it's different in the east from the kingdom, that your family name comes first. And your name's Yuui Laika, right? So then, I thought I wouldn't call you Yuui, if you didn't like it..."

Yuui was a little confused but turned to face him fully. With resolute motions, she drew right up next to him. When she was

©Enji

so close that their bodies nearly touched, she stood on her tiptoes and brought her face to his ear.

"Wh-what?" he asked.

In a whisper, she said, "My family has no surname. We go by our given name and, in the kingdom, a temporary name. The order matches kingdom order."

"So then, Laika is—?"

"In my case, it's my grandmother's name."

"...Uh-huh."

Yuui lowered herself and put a few steps' distance between them.

She smiled as she looked at him and said, "Though I don't mind if you wish to call me that."

"No..." He let out a slow sigh. "I'll just call you what I have been."

"All right," she said.

"I want a drink."

"Hmm? What does that mean?" She blinked in confusion but then smiled and bowed. "Take care, Ix."

"You too, Yuui."

Ix watched her and Nova disappear down the road. He still stood there even after they were gone from sight.

The air, waiting for the fast-approaching winter, chilled his cheeks.

He came back to himself and looked at the envelope in his hand. Tearing it open, he found a single sheet of high-quality paper. Nothing was written on the front, so he flipped it over.

Well-formed characters spelled out only two words: *Good work*.

A wry chuckle escaped his lips.

He thought back to what Yuui had said.

"What does that mean...?"

Yes, what did that mean...?

He decided that one day, he would tell her.

The noontime forest looked incredibly peaceful. Birdsong filled the air, tree branches rustled, and light dappled the forest floor.

Partway there, an enedo met him and showed him the rest of the way. As they approached the house, it let out a sound somewhat like a sneeze and disappeared into the forest.

She was there, standing on the roof of the house, looking straight up.

Her black coat fluttered, and her absurdly large hat seemed ready to tip over.

The weather was bright and clear that day, rare for the kingdom in fall. There was not a single cloud in the sky, which seemed like a pale-blue sheet that continued on forever. The sunshine was warm, and the wind was cool.

Ix noticed that a branch had been cut from each of the trees surrounding the clearing. There were sharp cross sections and light-colored incisions. They'd been cut from near the base of the tree, which made him think of a large bundle of sticks. Perhaps she had made a broom or something similar.

She noticed him and leaped to the ground.

"Hello," she said with a smile.

"The staff's done," he replied.

"That was fast. Wasn't it supposed to take half a year the first time?"

"That was because Master had other contracts to deal with at the shop. Most of the crafting time for your order was just waiting for those to be finished. But this time, yours was my one job."

"You really didn't want to make a different one?"

"I'm going to start now. I'd decided to focus entirely on the one that needed finishing before that... Actually, I couldn't even work on another staff while there was one sitting there unfinished. This whole time..."

"Really?" she said gently.

Ix set down his bag and pulled out a long, thin package.

He put on a pair of white gloves, then opened it with care. The outermost layer was cloth. Inside was a layer of paper, followed by another layer of cloth, this time an immaculate white that wrapped around the staff to protect it.

He undid the final cord, and the cloth slipped apart, revealing the staff.

It was bright in color, its length about from the ground to his chest. The core material in the top was a mix of gold and brown.

Ix slowly raised the staff with both hands and held it out to her.

She straightened her back and held out her hands as well.

"Engraved number: 3403, Passing. Made from the fourth branch of a reneel tree. The core is eshi amber. It is stubborn and gentle," he said quietly. "Crafter: Ix. Owner: Camilla Toah."

"Wrong."

"Huh?"

"I'm not Camilla anymore. I'm the witch," she said with a gentle smile.

"...Crafter: Ix. Owner: the witch."

"Mm-hmm."

The witch nodded and accepted the staff.

She took the staff, the first Ix had ever made, with such joy.

She poured some warm tea for him, which the two sipped as they sat outside. Ix didn't drink it immediately, as it was too hot.

"How did you figure it out, Ix?" asked the witch gently. "Even with what I am now, I still barely believe it. I don't think it's something a human would be capable of imagining."

"It's not like I understand how it works. I just realized the structure and told you about it."

"Incredible... And I never even suspected."

"I wanted to ask before, but it is magic, right?"

"Ummm... Keep this a secret from everyone else, okay? This is special." She winked. "A spell is a technique for changing mana into a variety of possible forms, right? There's heat, light, sound... But there are still so many things it can be turned into. Like...what should I call it...? Knowledge? Or perhaps it would be easier to understand if I call it information? You change the information you have into mana and release it. Obviously, the reverse is also possible."

The witch shrugged and continued.

"This was originally how the dragons gave humans knowledge. They couldn't convey everything with words, so they would give it in a single lump of information. But when that knowledge was just far too large for a human to take in...they used this forest."

"...The forest?"

"Yes. Mana flows through the trees of the woods, right? They put the information they couldn't all fit into their heads into the trees, so they could access it whenever they needed it. It's almost like the forest itself is one massive brain. That's why the witch has always lived here. We wouldn't want someone to come and cut down all the trees while she was away, now, would we?"

"Uh-huh...," Ix said, his eyes closed as he nodded.

Turning information into mana and releasing it...hmm.

If that was possible, there would be no need for schools or books.

Was this, too, a magic that humans would achieve in the distant future?

"Right, now it's your turn," said the witch with a smirk. "You didn't know anything about that kind of magic, so how did you figure out the...structure?"

Ix looked up at the sky and murmured, "Because Mali cried."

"That's why?"

"Well, it's not really the reason why, but it was a clue that led to the realization." He let out a sigh and explained. "First of all, why was Mali chased out of the forest sixty years ago? That confused me. If the witch was really a powerful magic user, she would never have allowed that. She would have immediately located Mali and gobbled her up. Which meant she couldn't do that. There was some reason why she couldn't eat her. Once I hit upon that, it led to only one probable explanation." He held up a finger. "The witch can't eat someone without their consent."

"That's what you thought…?"

"I had absolutely no idea why it was that way," continued Ix. "But as I thought about it, I realized I was making it too complicated. I was distracted by the immortality and the people eating and the mysterious witch. Even though anyone who thought about it logically would come to a simpler and more realistic answer…"

In all probability…

The reason he hadn't realized it was because he hadn't done it himself.

Ix took a sip of the tea and sighed. "Raising a successor who takes on their title. It's that simple. The witch raises a new witch, and that person becomes the next one. People die, but the witch is immortal. I hadn't determined exactly how it happened, but I figured this was the only way that made sense. Which is why I suggested that you be the next witch."

"…I don't understand why the first witch did that, though," she said falteringly. "But that's information I can learn. I do know that long ago, there was the festival, the Feast of Meat, and there was a child watching a ring of people dancing, unable to join. The witch took that child in, and ever since, the title has continued to be passed down." She smiled slightly there. "Oh yes, this hat… At some point, this odd tradition came about of giving an even bigger hat to the next witch than the hat you received when you took on the role. That's why it's so big."

Ix couldn't help but think that this was how it should be.

There were seven gravestones behind the house.

That was the number of people who had been eaten up until now.

Individuality discarded for the sake of a single name.

Immortality created for the sake of a single girl.

That's why they kept passing it on.

For an eternity...

They would pass down the witch.

The witch pressed a finger to her cheek and said, "Mali must have run away before she knew the truth..."

"She knew."

"Hmm?"

"There's no way she wouldn't come to such a simple conclusion in the twenty years she lived with the witch."

"Then why did she flee?"

"Because there's only one witch." Ix drew in a breath. "If she became the witch, the previous one would die. Mali was afraid of that, so she ran. That's why...she cried. And I'm sure the witch realized that, too. I don't know what kind of relationship those two built up over the course of twenty years, but...that's why the witch decided to let things end."

"Oh..."

The two exchanged silent glances.

Their tea had gone cold.

"What's she doing now? The old...uh," said Ix as he cocked his head. "What do I call her?"

"Ebe," said the witch with a smile. "Mm. She asked for some time, and she went to go visit Mali. Apparently, there's a bit of a delay once you pass on the witch."

"...Uh-huh." Ix imagined the white-haired elderly woman and the black-haired girl conversing.

"But she said she'd be back by winter to, mm, enter her grave."

"...The witch is cruel."

"...Yeah."

There was nothing else to say.

Before he left the forest, he stood face-to-face with the witch and said, "So, how long is it, then?"

"How long is what?"

"A witch's life span. It's probably longer than a normal human's, just not forever. The witch would need to look for her successor while keeping an eye on that span of time."

"Yeah… It's generally around two or three hundred years."

"So there really is a connection between mana and life span."

"…Yeah," confirmed the witch with a small nod.

"That a secret, too?"

"It is, but…" Her lips trembled. "Humans and magic beasts can naturally use magic to, uh, sort of replace what you might think of as your life energy. They can reduce the amount of life energy they use by substituting a bit of mana instead. That's why magic beasts with mana live longer than your normal beasts without it… That's…how it works."

"How much longer?"

"How much?" She tried to force a smile on her face.

"Or the opposite, how much shorter is it?"

The witch closed her eyes and shook her head.

Did she not know?

Or was that the one thing that would remain a secret?

She came closer to him, circled her arms around his back, and hugged him.

"I…," she said, her voice coming up from below because of their difference in height. "I am the witch. I know so much that humans don't. I can use magic that humans can't. You would be surprised if you knew the things I'm capable of. It makes you feel like you can do anything. But…what is this about? How can I be this sad, in this much pain, when the sky is this blue? Even though it was raining so hard not long ago…?"

"……"

"Ix, I met you when you were a baby." Her face was obscured

by the large brim of her hat. "I tried to give you a flower. Why did I do that? I don't know, but I tried to make you hold it in your right hand. You cried. You seemed unhappy. But I kept pressing it into your hand, over and over, trying to force your little hand to take the flower. I'm...so sorry... I'm sorry, Ix..."

He didn't understand why she was apologizing like this, but then he thought, *Ah, she's the witch.*

She was apologizing for something that happened twenty years ago as though it had happened yesterday.

No human could do that, not unless they were somehow special.

That's why she was meant to become the witch.

At the same time, he felt a sort of understanding about something. That was it...

It was from all the way back then...

No wonder he couldn't disobey anything she'd said...

She pressed her face into his chest for a while. Then she released him and looked up with a smiling face.

In a cheerful voice so different from before, she said, "By the way, Ebe flies."

"She flies?"

"Yeah, she said she was going to fly to Leirest. She left while I was sleeping, though, so I don't know how..."

"But you're the witch."

"I told you—there's too much information to sift through. I've got my hands full just finding what's where."

"Is that so."

"It is so. Oh, but," she said in an amused tone, "there are the sticks."

"Huh?"

"It's weird... For some reason, she cut a bunch of branches over there. No idea what she's using them for, though...," she said and smiled.

Ix followed her eyes into the sky.

©Enji

To the place that she, too, would someday go.

A height that he couldn't achieve in his entire life.

The next day, Ix heard rumors of a person soaring through the sky.

Apparently, someone had caught sight of a human figure at night cutting across the white moon.

That black shadow cast in front of the moon had a pointed hat and rode a broom.

━━ Afterword ━━

Every reader has the liberty to decide where they start reading or where they stop reading. However, just as stories are rarely constructed with the assumption that you will start reading them from the end, I write this afterword with the presumption that it will be read last (there are crucial spoilers). Please understand. It's easier to just copy and paste this.

The title of this book is *Dragon and Ceremony 2: The Passing of the Witch*, but *Dragon and Ceremony* was the title made for the content of the previous book, so it would be more accurate to call this book simply *The Passing of the Witch*. Or, if we're sticking to the same format, maybe *Witch and Meat*. That sounds a bit macabre, though, so let's just not.

As I said, this is the second book in the series, a direct sequel to *Dragon and Ceremony: From a Wandmaker's Perspective*. It's set in the same world and takes place after the events in the first volume. However, both this volume and the previous entry were each wrapped up within their respective pages, so it's not a problem if you read this one first or if it's the only one you read (though I feel there aren't too many people who would do that).

I wrote this book in October and November of 2019, and it took just over four weeks. I spent the first two weeks writing the first half, then deleting it. I spent the remaining two weeks and change rewriting the whole thing from scratch. That's how I scheduled it. This was my first time writing a sequel. To be honest, I'd actually planned to finish with the last volume. I think that was why I ran into so many issues. At one point, I might have asked, "Can I leave Yuui out of Volume Two?" to which I got the reproaching response of, "No, it's a light novel…"

It's a good thing I didn't start by asking, "Can I change the main character?"

One difference from the previous volume is that this story is primarily set in lively places with large crowds. There is generally an atmosphere of excitement and busyness, which might heighten the sense of a festival. The "inside and outside" key words make an appearance in this book as well. And then there may have been some performances by the cast that I used to mislead the readers, but…we'll leave that there.

Since it is a series, this volume shares some themes with the previous entry, but the approach is different. Readers might have felt some difference in that regard. On the content side, it also contains some counters and answers to the first volume. That is to say, it's like the relationship between point A and point B. If I had to boil them down to one word, I would say the first volume was about *records* while the second volume is about *emotions* (that's the crucial spoiler).

Just like Volume 1, I wrote Volume 2 with the intention of ending things there, but to my complete surprise, I am now planning on putting out a third volume. It will be set in winter.

April 2020, Ichimei Tsukushi